TWO Boys BY THE POND

AF660560

VIVEK MOHAN

BlueRose ONE .com
Stories Matter
New Delhi • London

BLUEROSE PUBLISHERS
India | U.K.

BlueRose ONE
Stories Matter
NewDelhi • London

For permissions requests or inquiries regarding this publication, please contact:

BLUEROSE PUBLISHERS
www.BlueRoseONE.com
info@bluerosepublishers.com
+91 8882 898 898
+4407342408967

ISBN: 978-93-7310-211-5

Cover design: Daksh
Typesetting: Tanya Raj Upadhyay

First Edition: September 2025

Dedication

To Ethan Noah,

My brightest star and the softest part of my world.

May you always grow with kindness in your heart, wonder in your eyes, and the courage to be wholly, unapologetically yourself.

Preface

Some stories are not imagined; they are remembered. They live in the quiet corners of our hearts, waiting to be told, not for their grandeur, but for the truth they hold about love, longing, and loss.

This novel is spun together from real incidents from my adolescence and my partner's. Though we didn't know each other back then, I wove our memories into a single thread, creating a story that carries both our truths.

In writing this, I wanted to preserve the fragile beauty of love in its purest form, the kind that thrives in secrecy yet shines brighter than anything spoken aloud. It is also a story of grief, of what happens when love is left unfinished, and yet, in memory, becomes eternal.

I hope as you turn these pages, you too can feel the weight of silence, the warmth of a hidden smile, and the ache of knowing that sometimes, love is both the gift and the wound.

Acknowledgements

To Shahir—

For being my inspiration, my anchor, and my quiet strength through it all.

Thank you for your unwavering patience, your love that held me gently, and your constant support as I brought this story to life.

This wouldn't exist without you.

Always grateful.

Always yours.

Table of Contents

Chapter 1: The Road to Palakkad

Morning sunlight filtered through the gauzy curtains, painting golden stripes across Gokul's modest bedroom. Gokul was tall, with broad shoulders that gave the illusion of athleticism, but his body was soft from months of sitting indoors, buried in textbooks and screens. His brown complexion caught the morning light, and his large, expressive eyes often revealed the thoughts he tried to hide. His hair, long and unruly since the board exams, fell messily over his forehead—a silent rebellion against routine. Though not unfit, his frame lacked the firmness of activity. Gokul sat cross-legged on his neatly made bed, suitcase open at his feet, clothes half-folded inside.

For months, the pressure had been unrelenting. Entrance exams loomed like dark clouds on the horizon, board exams followed closely behind, and the constant whispers of "excel, achieve, outperform" buzzed in his ears. His diary—once an outlet for his deepest thoughts—had been gathering dust on his shelf. Every page held confessions and anxieties he wasn't ready to share, even with himself.

He reached out to pick up the diary, fingertips brushing the cool cover. But then he hesitated. This fortnight in his grandparents' village—Palakkad—was supposed to be a true break. A chance to leave everything behind: the textbooks, the deadlines, and the unspoken secret that gnawed at him from within. Gokul closed the diary and placed it back on the desk. Some stories, he decided, were better left unwritten for now.

His mother's voice drifted up from the courtyard below. "Are you ready, mone?" she called, a hint of excitement in her tone.

"Almost," he replied, zipping up his suitcase. With one last glance around the room, he took a deep breath, feeling a rare sense of peace settle in his chest.

***

Gokul climbed down the stairs slowly, his fingertips grazing the railing. The air felt still, and it seemed as though the morning light hadn't quite reached the ground floor yet. Shadows stretched along the walls, soft and quiet. From the far end of the hall, a warm yellow glow spilled from the dining room.

His mother, Latha sat at the table, waiting for him, still in her cotton night salwar, her hair tied up in a loose bun. A bowl of steaming oats rested in front of his usual chair, the steam curling upward, carrying the mild aroma of cinnamon and dry fruits.

"Good morning, mone," she said, her voice low but cheerful, almost like she had been waiting for him to arrive so her day could begin properly.

"Morning, Amma."

He slid into the chair, still a little sleepy, and eyed the bowl in front of him. Oats—again. He wasn't the biggest fan, but over the years, he'd gotten used to them. They were healthy, and deep down, Gokul was always a little too conscious of his health, the way his body looked, and how his skin felt during the stress of exams. So, he ate them.

His mother noticed the hesitation. "I know, I know," she smiled. "But I added extra nuts today. Almonds, pistachios... a few raisins too. That should help you forgive me?"

Gokul chuckled, taking a bite. "You're lucky I like pistachios."

She reached out and brushed his hair back from his forehead. "You look tired. Didn't sleep well?"

"Just... couldn't switch off my head. I kept thinking about... everything." He shrugged, not going into detail.

His mother didn't press. Instead, she rested her hand on his and said gently, "It's okay to take a break. Even your mind deserves a vacation. Don't overthink this trip. Just be there. Enjoy. Let your grandparents spoil you."

He nodded, swallowing the next spoonful. "Thanks, Amma."

Just then, footsteps echoed from the hallway. His father, Suresh, emerged from the bedroom, stifling a yawn. Tall and broad-shouldered, with his signature pleated pants and a tucked-in shirt even this early, he looked alert as always, though his eyes were still adjusting to the light.

"Oh! You're up early, acha," Gokul said, surprised.

"I thought I'd see you off," his father replied, walking over to the table. "How often do you leave for two weeks, hmm?"

Gokul smiled. "Not very."

His father placed a hand on his shoulder—a brief, solid gesture. "Palakkad isn't Kochi. Be respectful. Listen to your grandparents. Don't be on your phone all the time. Help them if they ask. Understood?"

"Yes, Acha." Gokul tried not to roll his eyes, but he appreciated the concern buried beneath the instruction.

His father gave a small nod. "And if Ammama makes that bitter herbal thing again, just drink it. Don't make faces."

Now Gokul did laugh. "No promises."

His mother chuckled. "He'll manage. He's not a little boy anymore."

Gokul stood, picking up his bag and slinging it over his shoulder. He leaned in toward his mother, wrapping his arms around her in a warm, lingering embrace. She held him tightly, kissing his forehead and brushing his back gently, as if trying to pass on a little more strength before he left.

Then his father stepped forward and placed a firm hand on his back. "I'll drop you at the bus stand," he said, already reaching for his keys.

But Gokul shook his head. "Achaa... it's okay. I'll go alone. This trip—it has to be done alone."

For a second, his father studied him, eyes narrowing slightly. Gokul held his gaze—not defiantly, but with a quiet determination.

Finally, his father sighed and gave a small nod, the way someone does when they know their child has outgrown something—this time, perhaps the need to be walked to the gate. "Alright," he said, voice softer than before. "Go safe. And call once you reach."

Gokul nodded. And with that, Gokul stepped out the door, the soft morning air brushing against his face. He was leaving with more than a suitcase—he carried with him the quiet strength of his mother's care, and the solid presence of his father's steady hand.

***

The taxi ride to the railway station was smooth, the early-morning streets of Kochi surprisingly quiet. Gokul stared out the window at the waking city—coffee shops opening their doors, office-goers hurrying along, digital billboards flickering to life. It all felt distant, like a dream he was leaving behind.

Gokul boarded the train from the platform. His grandparents were waiting in a village on the far edge of Palakkad, where time moved differently—slower, gentler. No constant notifications, no push to be the best. Just rustling palm trees, the call of the koel at dawn, and endless fields of paddy whispering in the breeze.

The train chugged forward, carrying Gokul away from his routines and the expectations that came with them. He sank into his seat and closed his eyes. For the first time in months, his mind wasn't racing with formulas, study schedules, or that secret he feared might unravel him.

Behind his eyelids, he pictured his grandmother's smile, the aroma of her freshly brewed filter coffee, the feel of soft earth under his feet as he helped his grandfather in the courtyard. He imagined nights spent under a canopy of stars, swapping stories around a crackling fire, laughter echoing between the banana trees.

Gokul exhaled slowly, a small smile tugging at the corners of his mouth. This was the escape he needed—the place where he could simply be himself, without the weight of "what ifs" and "should haves." As the train gathered speed, he realized that sometimes, the greatest journeys begin when you dare to close your diary and let the world write the next chapter.

Chapter 2: Green and Gold

Gokul alighted at Palakkad station, the dry summer heat immediately wrapping around him like a dusty shawl. The air smelled of warm stone, coconut oil, and the faint tang of iron rails. He walked past rows of vendors and sleepy passengers, dragging his small suitcase behind him, its wheels bumping unevenly over the cracked platform tiles.

Gokul walked to the bus terminal, 100 meters down the road, where he found a rickety old bus idling in the corner—its paint faded, lettering half-worn, as if time had gently rubbed against it over the years. The conductor barely looked up as Gokul boarded. The bus was nearly empty, save for an old man chewing betel nut near the window and a woman in a bright green saree whispering into her phone.

As the engine sputtered to life and the bus rolled forward with a groan, Gokul felt a soft wave of memory wash over him. The same journey, years ago—only then he had been nestled between his parents, their voices low and warm, pointing out buffaloes and temple spires through the window. His mother had packed lemon rice wrapped in banana leaf, and his father had reminded him not to lean too far out the window. He smiled faintly at the memory.

The landscape blurred past, green and gold—fields of paddy stretched endlessly on either side, palm trees swaying like they were gossiping with the wind. A white heron stood in the middle of a flooded field, motionless and regal.

But as the road curved past an old bridge, something inside Gokul shifted. A flicker of unease stirred in his chest—something he couldn't name. A memory, perhaps. A feeling he had tried to bury. It caught him off guard, tugging at the edge of his thoughts like an old scar pressed too hard.

He shifted in his seat and looked away from the fields. *Not now,* he told himself. *Not today.* He wasn’t ready to unpack the past, not when he had come all this way to forget it.

Instead, he let the bus rock him gently, its old body creaking with every turn. He closed his eyes for a moment and decided to surrender—to the moment, to the heat, to the smell of wet earth and distant smoke, to the quiet of a village that didn't care about marks or medals or secrets he hadn't yet learned to name.

He would reach soon. And maybe, just maybe, the peace he was looking for would be waiting at the other end of the road.

***

The bus dropped Gokul off at a narrow turn where the tarred road thinned into gravel. He walked the last few meters, dragging his suitcase through the crunch of dry leaves and tiny stones. And then he saw it—his grandparents' house, standing just as he remembered it, yet worn gently by time.

It was an old, one-storey terrace house, designed in the late 80s, with faint hints of its former charm still clinging to the pink exterior. The paint had faded unevenly under the Palakkad sun, weathered and chipped in places, giving it a muted, rose-dust color. Moss had crept up along the edges, stubborn and green. But the front yard was alive—a riot of plants, tall and short, potted and wild, with hibiscus flowers in bloom, bougainvillaea spilling over the boundary wall, and a few overenthusiastic creepers climbing the grill of the veranda.

On the wide veranda, two familiar figures stood waiting—his grandmother, Lakshmi, in a loose cream-colored blouse and pink floral saree, wiping her hands on the end of her towel, and his grandfather, Aravind, a thin man in a faded checked lungi and a grey polo t-shirt, clutching a folded newspaper under his arm.

"Gokule, how long has it been da!" his grandmother exclaimed, her eyes crinkling with joy. Before he could even drop his bag, she wrapped him in a tight, warm embrace, smelling of sandalwood powder and kitchen smoke.

"Look at you," she said, pulling back to examine his face. "You've become so thin! Are they not feeding you in that city?"

His grandfather smiled, more reserved, but his eyes shone. He placed a hand on Gokul's shoulder. "Long journey, ah? Come, come. Inside. Your Ammamma's been cooking like you're bringing an army."

Before he could protest, his grandmother had already dragged him through the cool tiled corridor, chattering all the way about the sweets she'd made "just this morning."

The living room still had the same cane chairs, the old wall clock that ticked loudly, and the scent of agarbatti lingering faintly in the corners. Gokul sat down at the table as a plate appeared in front of him—golden brown *unniyappams*, crisp and warm, and delicate *achappams* that crumbled with the lightest bite. She poured him a steel tumbler of tea, the kind that was perfectly sweet, milky, and spiced with cardamom.

“This... this is magic,” Gokul said between mouthfuls.

His grandmother beamed. “Eat more. I’ll make you proper meals here.”

After finishing his tea and a quick call to his mother to let her know he’d reached safely, Lakshmi gently guided Gokul down the side corridor to his room—the same one that had once belonged to his father. The wooden door creaked open, revealing a space frozen in a simpler time. The walls had old movie posters peeling at the corners, a wooden desk by the window, and a bed covered in a soft, faded cotton sheet.

Gokul walked over to the window. It opened to a breathtaking view—the backyard sloped down to a quiet stream that shimmered in the sunlight, and beyond it stretched the familiar paddy fields, lush and green, dancing gently in the breeze.

He placed his suitcase by the wall, and flopped onto the bed. The mattress dipped with a comforting familiarity. The ceiling fan whirred softly above, slow and rhythmic.

For the first time in weeks, maybe months, Gokul let out a full breath—not one held back by deadlines or expectations. Just a quiet, content sigh.

Here, in this small pink house with creaking floors and cardamom tea, he felt something he hadn't felt in a long time.

Peace.

***

When Gokul opened his eyes, the light had shifted. A soft orange hue spilled through the slits in the wooden window, and the fan above him spun lazily in the late afternoon air. It was already 5 PM. He had slept deeper than he expected, his body finally surrendering to rest after months of running on adrenaline and willpower.

He quickly stepped into the living room where the smell of fried banana chips and fresh tea instantly lifted his mood.

"Ammamma, that smells too good," he said, sitting on the wooden stool by the open kitchen doorway.

His grandmother smiled, placing a tumbler of tea and a plate of *kaaya varuthathu* on the table. "Your grandfather's been talking all afternoon about the jackfruit in Anandan's backyard. Says he's going to ask for one tomorrow."

"Our Mangoes too," Gokul added, taking a sip of tea. "Are they still the sour kind?"

"Oh yes," Ammamma laughed. "You used to cry when we made you eat those raw slices with salt."

"Still do," Gokul grinned.

Just then, his grandfather walked in from the front yard, wiping sweat off his forehead. "I'm telling you, this year that jackfruit is the size of a gas cylinder. We're getting it before the squirrels do."

They chuckled, falling into the kind of light-hearted village banter that was both grounding and comforting. After some more chit-chat and seconds of tea, Gokul excused himself.

"I think I'll go check out the backyard. Maybe take a dip."

Ammamma called after him, "Take your towel and come back before it gets dark. The mosquitoes don't show mercy here!"

He grabbed his towel, slung it around his shoulder, and walked barefoot to the back of the house. The evening sun was still warm, casting a golden sheen across the tall grass and fluttering leaves. The path was overgrown in places, but still familiar—his feet instinctively finding their way down the gentle slope.

The stream glistened just as he remembered—calm, clear, and cool. On the other side, the paddy fields stretched endlessly, soaking in the orange sky.

By the bank, Gokul undressed slowly, folding his clothes onto a dry patch of rock. His body, though soft from disuse, still held the faint outlines of a boy who once ran through school fields and did crunches before exams. The months had left their marks—tired shoulders, a slouched back—but something in the air, the water, the stillness, started to ease it all.

He waded in. The stream embraced him like a lullaby, cool and fluid, wrapping around his body and washing away a little more of the weight he'd carried in silence. He tilted his head back, letting the water trail down his spine.

Then, from across the stream, a voice—soft, but distinct.

"You do remember me, right?"

Gokul turned, startled for a moment. Standing at the edge on the other side was a tall boy, wearing a navy blue T-shirt and rolled-up pants. His face was pale, almost luminescent in the twilight, with eyes that carried both shyness and sharp curiosity.

Gokul blinked. Then a small smile crept onto his lips. "Taher?"

The boy smiled faintly, and nodded.

They stood there for a moment, just looking—two boys with years between them, and yet something about the moment made it feel like they had never really been apart.

"I didn't think you'd remember," Taher said, shifting his weight.

"I couldn't forget," Gokul replied. "You were the only friend I ever had here."

Taher laughed softly. "We used to play cricket with a coconut branch, remember? You always cheated."

"And you always let me win," Gokul smirked.

The sun dipped lower, and a sudden gust of wind rustled through the distant plantain. Taher looked toward the sky.

"It's getting late," he said, stepping back. "Let's meet tomorrow?"

Gokul nodded. "Yeah. Tomorrow."

And just like that, Taher turned and disappeared into the green, leaving behind only his faint footprints in the mud and something stirring in Gokul's chest–something quiet, familiar, and yet entirely new.

***

After talking with his parents over the phone–his mother asking if he remembered to drink enough water, and his father reminding him again to help out around the house–Gokul smiled and nodded through their concern. But before he could wrap up the call with another "I'm fine, Amma," he heard his grandmother's familiar voice calling from the kitchen, "kazhikan vaa da, Gokule!"

Dinner time.

He quickly cut the call and leapt out of bed, his body still groggy from the journey, but his nose already catching the rich aroma floating through the house. It was unmistakable—his favourite *varutharacha kozhi curry*.

The dining room, dimly lit by a single tube light and the warm glow from the kitchen, felt like a soft cocoon of memories. His grandfather was already seated, arms crossed, pretending to look stern, though his eyes warmed when he saw Gokul.

"Come, come. You must be starving," he said, motioning to the seat beside him.

Gokul grinned and slid into the wooden chair, his stomach grumbling in agreement. He scooped a generous portion of steaming white rice onto his plate as his grandmother shuffled over with a ladle full of thick, spiced chicken curry.

"There's more in the pot. Don't be shy," she said, pouring it over the rice with a love only grandmothers could measure.

The curry was rich, roasted coconut mingling with the deep spices, and it tasted exactly like his childhood summers—like stories, like safety. Between mouthfuls, they chatted about the neighbour's runaway goat, the mangoes that would soon be ready to pluck, and the heavy rains expected the coming week.

After seconds (and thirds), Gokul leaned back in his chair, completely full and deeply content. The grandparents, like clockwork, retired to bed soon after, switching off lights and securing the doors with the gentle routine of people who had done it for decades.

Gokul, however, wasn't sleepy yet.

He went back to his room, shut the door gently behind him, and flopped back onto the cotton bed. The night air was cooler now. He pulled out his phone and, like clockwork too, opened Instagram. Just a quick scroll, he told himself.

A few messages, a few memes, some harmless scrolling.

Then—*him*.

His once best friend. The one who used to sit next to him in class. Who waited for him after tuition. Who knew every stupid inside joke and every silent worry.

Now, just a name on a screen. A face surrounded by new people. New friends. Apparently, they had a small meet-up. Gokul hadn't even heard about it.

He tapped through the stories, one by one, each frame feeling like a quiet punch to the gut. How did things change so fast? How could someone who once knew your mind inside-out now treat you like just another follower?

He stared at the ceiling for a while, phone resting on his chest. Then, with a tired sigh, he locked the screen and turned over to face the window.

No—tonight wasn't the night to unearth old secrets.

The moonlight poured in, silvering the edge of the table, the wall, and the floor. Outside, the crickets chirped like a lullaby, and the silence of the village wrapped around him like a blanket.

It didn't fix anything. But it helped. Just a little.

And with that calmness gently settling into his bones, Gokul finally let his eyes close, the weight of the city slowly dissolving into the quiet of the village night.

Chapter 3 - The Way Back

Mornings in the village were something else. The kind that made you believe the world hadn't gone entirely wrong. Sunlight filtered through the canopy of trees, soft and golden. The koel's calls danced with the chirping of smaller birds. The air smelt of hibiscus, wet earth, and something sweet he couldn't place—maybe it was peace.

Gokul stepped barefoot into the backyard, letting the cool soil kiss his soles. He had missed this—missed it deeply. Kochi, with all its buzz and brightness, never gave him this kind of silence. Not the good kind. Not the kind that hugged you without asking questions.

The stream behind the house, once wild and proud, was now tamed—lined with a rough concrete path on either side. He walked along its bank, touching familiar trees like they were old friends: Mohanettan's jackfruit tree, its huge fruit drooping under its own weight; Amritha chechi's mango tree, the one with the sugary-sweet *priyoor* variety they used to steal during the neighborhood wandering.

As he walked, his mind travelled back to summers long gone. The little bridge came into view—a small, arched one connecting both banks of the stream. He smiled. That bridge was more than just stone and cement; it was memory itself. Beyond it lay Taher's house.

He was there, right on cue.

Taher sat cross-legged on the veranda, draped in his usual maroon tee and black trackpants, a book open in his lap. His hair, damp from a recent bath, was neatly pushed back, a little flower tucked behind one ear—perhaps unconsciously. His fingers traced the pages absentmindedly, and when he looked up, his eyes lit up.

"Still the same Gokul?" Taher called out with a small grin.

"And you? Still dressing like a campus poet?" Gokul teased.

Taher laughed, brushing the flower away with a flick that was almost theatrical. "What to do, I have a reputation to maintain."

Before Gokul could say more, Taher's mother's voice rang out from inside, sharp but affectionate: "*Taher, Is that Gokul? Did he reach safe? Ask him about his exams!*"

"She's obsessed with exams," Taher muttered, half-smiling, then louder: "Ummachi, he passed everything. Even the stress test."

From inside came a sigh, followed by, "Good. Now give him tea. Black, and strong."

Taher disappeared inside briefly and returned with two steel tumblers. "She thinks tea can fix the world," he said, handing one to Gokul.

"Sometimes it does," Gokul said, taking a sip. It was hot and sharp, like a slap that woke you up in a good way.

***

After the tea, they started walking.

The path was still the same, bending gently past wild bushes and a line of old stone markers half-buried in the grass. Gokul's eyes lit up when he spotted something crimson near the base of a gulmohar tree.

"Manjadi!" he exclaimed, dropping to his knees.

He scooped the red seeds into his palm, like a little boy discovering treasure. "I used to carry these around like they were gold coins."

"We used to play with it as coins, remember that?", Taher said, shaking his head with a grin.

"Oh, yeah!" Gokul nodded, tucking the seeds into his pocket, like he was storing a piece of childhood.

Soon they reached the pond.

It was still as a mirror, framed by mossy stone steps and guarded by tall *nirmalyam* trees. A forgotten little paradise. They sat on the steps, side by side, legs stretched out.

"This place..." Gokul exhaled. "Feels like it's been waiting for us."

Taher smiled, hugging his knees. "You remember the time you slipped and fell in?"

"Oh god," Gokul groaned, hiding his face. "I thought I was going to drown in three feet of water."

"You cried so much I thought your lungs would give up before the water did," Taher giggled, his fingers curling over his lips delicately.

Gokul smiled despite himself. "And you... you were so scared, you just stood there holding that stupid catapult."

"Hey! That catapult got us mangoes."

"True." Gokul stretched his legs and leaned back. "Amritha chechi would still be talking about her 'mango thief'. I always took the blame."

They burst into laughter again, easy and unguarded.

"This place hasn't changed," Gokul said, softly. "But everything else has."

Taher was quiet for a moment, tracing the edge of a step with his finger.

"I'm learning tailoring now," he said. "From the co-op centre in town. I want to do fashion design. Maybe even start a label."

Gokul turned to him, surprised but delighted. "Really?"

"Yeah," Taher said, eyes lighting up. "I'm not great at academics. But with fabric, with colours... I feel like myself."

There was something about the way he said it—firm, proud, yet unspokenly vulnerable. Gokul admired that. The quiet courage.

"You'll be great at it," he said. "I mean it."

They sat in silence for a while. The pond shimmered under the late morning sun. A dragonfly hovered close before darting off. Gokul traced a pattern on the moss with his toe.

"I needed this, Taher," he said. "The calm. The air. Just... this."

"Bad days?"

"Bad months," Gokul admitted. "Exams. Expectations. It all felt like a chokehold."

He was about to say more—about Jobin, the friend who left without a word, who carved a hollow in his chest—but something in him held back.

Not today.

So instead, he sighed and said, "I think I'll survive this summer."

Taher looked at him, resting his cheek on his hand. "You will."

Gokul smiled.

The wind rustled through the trees, the pond reflected their shared stillness, and somewhere far away, a koel called again—as if it, too, remembered.

Chapter 4: Twin Flame

Back then, they said Gokul and Jobin were inseparable.

If you saw one walking across the corridor, the other was not far behind—usually with a shared smirk or some ongoing conversation that made sense only to them. They sat together, ate together, bunked morning assemblies together. Even the teachers gave up eventually and called them "the twins."

Final year of higher secondary felt like the edge of a cliff. Everyone was preparing to jump off into adult life. But the two of them? They held on to the present like it was gold dust.

"Bro, I'm telling you—this year we'll crack the science fair. First prize or nothing," Jobin had said, chewing on the end of his pen.

Gokul nodded. "Let's make a working model this time. Not some volcano nonsense."

"Oh, now you remember the volcano? That was your idea."

"Yeah, and your baking soda ruined my shoes."

They sat cross-legged in the physics lab, glue stains on their hands, wires tangled between their knees. They made a model of a smart irrigation system, even though neither of them truly understood how sensors worked. What they did know was how to finish each other's sentences and split a Mazza during the breaks.

Lunch breaks were sacred. Gokul brought curd rice. Jobin brought chicken and rice. They always swapped the last bite.

Some days they stayed back after class, sitting under the huge mango tree near the basketball court, scribbling nonsense in each other's notebooks and talking about their crushes, their future college plans, their fear of leaving this bubble.

"I think you'll leave this place before I do," Jobin had said one day, out of the blue.

"Why would I?" Gokul asked, staring at the sunlight through the banyan leaves.

"You always wanted more. I think that's good. But it also means... you'll have to go far."

Gokul didn't know what to say then. He had laughed it off. "Then come with me."

But Jobin just smiled, soft and distant. "Some of us are built for the spotlight. Some of us are stagehands. And that's okay."

They had their fights, too. Short ones. Like the time Gokul lost his temper over a bad exam and snapped at Jobin for not calling the night before. Or when Jobin got too close to someone else and Gokul sulked for days. But no matter how messy things got, by the end of the day, they always found each other again.

There were days it felt like they were falling in love with life together.

But then the board exams came, and silence slowly crept in where conversations used to live.

Gokul, even now, wasn't ready to trace that silence to its root. He still searched for answers.

***

Gokul closed the book he'd been pretending to read for the past half hour. The pages had words, sure, but his eyes kept brushing past them, unfocused, circling back again and again—like his thoughts. He placed the book gently on the side table, its cover thudding soft against the wood.

The room was quiet, save for the distant hum of cicadas and the occasional rustle of leaves outside. But inside him, there was noise. A rising wave of thoughts he hadn't prepared for.

It was always Jobin.

Unresolved. Unspoken. Unsettling.

He thought this trip to the village would be his escape—into birdsong mornings and river-bathed afternoons. But Jobin had followed him here, not in person, but in memory. In ache. In everything that was left unsaid.

Why did they drift apart?

Was it something Gokul had done? Or... did Jobin suspect something?

That thought—that awful, tugging fear—tightened in his chest. Did Jobin know his secret? Had he sensed something that Gokul couldn't yet name back then?

A knot formed in his stomach.

No. No, it wasn't supposed to matter anymore. This was his time to breathe. To feel light. To leave it behind.

But the past always found its way back. And Gokul, no matter how far he ran, hadn't yet found a way to outrun Jobin's absence.

His throat went dry. A faint panic began rising in him, slow and warm like fever.

And then–

"Pazhampori undu, vaa mone!"

His grandmother's voice floated in from the kitchen, sunlit and perfectly timed.

He blinked, like surfacing from underwater. That's all it took–one familiar call, sweet and grounding–to pull him back to the now.

He stood up too fast, almost knocking over the glass of water on the table. But he didn't care. He was ready for the distraction. The scent of fried bananas and cardamom had already found its way to his door.

In the verandah, Lakshmi amma sat with a plate full of golden pazhampori and two cups of steaming tea beside her. Gokul's grandfather, folded neatly into the old cane chair, smiled the moment he saw him.

"Eat, eat before it gets cold," his grandmother fussed, adjusting her sari's pallu as she placed another piece on his plate.

Gokul smiled–finally, really smiled–and sat down.

This was exactly what he needed. A pause. A moment untouched by memory. Just the crunch of pazhampori and the warmth of tea shared with people who simply loved him.

The past could wait. For now, he had this.

After polishing off the last bite of pazhampori, Gokul stretched his legs out, let the tea warm his throat, and leaned back. The sky had turned honey-gold, the kind of colour that makes everything feel a little more possible.

He needed to go out. He wasn't sure why—but something inside him stirred, like a current asking to move.

"I'm heading out for a bit," he called to his grandmother as he slipped into his sandals.

"Okay mone, don't be too late. Take the umbrella," she said, even though the sky was spotless.

He didn't.

This time, he didn't take the winding way through the backyard and around the pond. Gokul walked straight—right through the side lane, past the old jackfruit tree, through the narrow path where the hibiscus leaves brushed his arm—and reached Taher's gate.

The front door was open, and Taher was crouched on the verandah fixing something on his cycle. His maroon tee had tiny grease stains on the side, and he looked up with a flash of surprise.

"Hey, enthada?" Taher smiled, wiping his hands on a cloth.

“Cycle ride?” Gokul asked casually, trying not to sound too eager. “Need to get a sketchbook and some pencils. You coming?”

Taher grinned and gave a small nod. “Wait, I’ll get my wallet.”

“You won’t need it,” Gokul said, and smirked.

They took Taher’s old Hero cycle—the same one from years ago, still rusted near the handles. Gokul hopped onto the front bar, feet resting on the axle bolts, hands lightly gripping the side of the handle.

As they started pedaling down the dusty village road, the wind ruffled Gokul’s unkempt hair. The air smelled of evening dust and jasmine from nearby fences—but what lingered most was Taher.

He smelled faintly sweet. Like guava ripening in the sun. Something warm. Familiar. Comforting.

Gokul closed his eyes for a second, just to feel the warmth on his skin. It had been a while since he felt this kind of calm. This kind of closeness.

Not since Jobin.

The market road wasn’t far. A few shops lined the main square, most of them small—steel containers rattling with toffees, weighing scales, old men reading newspapers by counters.

They reached the stationery shop with the blue shutter half rolled up. Inside, it smelled of paper, ink, and glue.

Gokul asked the man, "Oru drawing book undavoo? And HB pencil?"

The shopkeeper pulled out a medium-sized sketchbook with a butterfly on the cover. "I'll take two," Gokul said, placing them on the counter. He picked up a pair of pencils too.

Taher raised an eyebrow. "Two?"

"One for you," Gokul said, handing it to him. "To draw your designs. You told me, remember? That you wanted to be a designer."

Taher hesitated. "But... I can get mine later. Why waste your money—"

"Not a waste," Gokul interrupted softly. "Just... promise me you'll draw in it. I want to see the pages when they're full."

Taher looked down at the sketchbook in his hands. A single tear slipped down his cheek before he could blink it away.

"Hey..." Gokul reached out instinctively, gave a soft pat on Taher's back. "No crying. Or I'll start crying too, and we'll have to buy tissues next."

Taher let out a small laugh, nodding, wiping his eyes with the back of his hand. "Okay. Promise."

They rode back slower, the breeze cooler now, the sun dipping lower.

That evening, there was no silence between them—just the sound of wheels turning, hearts a little fuller, and two sketchbooks waiting to be filled.

***

After kissing his grandparents goodnight—his grandmother's arms still warm from the final hug, Gokul retired to his room.

His stomach was still heavy with all the love that came in the form of rice, sambar, beetroot thoran, and that perfect rasam his grandmother had perfected over the years. But his heart? That was heavier—with something far softer.

It felt good to be there. In that pink house with its withered walls and green spilling from every corner. In the slow, golden silence of the village, where even the night breeze whispered, instead of howled.

Gokul pulled out his phone, almost reluctantly. It had been a while since he touched it. His screen time had gone down without him even trying—something about the paddy fields and jasmine-scented air didn't need a digital distraction.

He unlocked the screen. A few notifications blinked. Nothing urgent.

Then he opened his photos, the recent ones. Most of them were casual—moments frozen without much thought. But when he paused at a picture from the market ride earlier that evening—him on the front bar, and Taher behind, his face partly in focus—he lingered.

Taher.

There was something about him. In those photos, his body was still and calm, but his eyes always carried a certain softness. His fingers in the frame looked delicate, like they had more practice holding a pencil than a hammer. Slightly effeminate, yes—but beautifully so. There was a quiet grace to the way he stood, the way he smiled, the way his shoulder tilted just enough, unintentionally.

Gokul stared at the picture longer than he meant to.

And then it hit him—that memory. The cycle ride. Taher's breath close to the nape of his neck, the warmth of his chest gently pressing behind him, the faint scent of something sweet—like guava ripening in the sun and warm skin. The way their laughs had synced for a moment, like they belonged to the same echo.

Gokul felt it. A soft flutter. Deep in his stomach, climbing up his throat, making his heart pound with a rhythm it hadn't known in a while.

A feeling he felt only while with Jobin, but stronger.

He smiled. A wide, helpless, almost embarrassed smile.

Without thinking much, Gokul posted a few photos to his story. Added a few hearts. Maybe too many. He didn't care.

He placed the phone on the table, the screen dimming quietly behind him. Then he rolled over on the cotton bed, cuddled the pillow close, burying his face into it.

The smell of starch and old wood filled his lungs while the fruity scent of guava ripening in the sun filled his heart.

Gokul closed his eyes.

And smiled.

Chapter 5: Where the Stream bends

The morning sun slanted through the gulmohar branches, casting lazy shadows on the stone steps by the pond. Gokul sat hunched, his sketchbook resting on his knees, a pencil lightly gripped in his right hand. A soft breeze moved the water in slow ripples, and the red petals from the gulmohar above floated down now and then—some landing on the pond, some on his shoulder.

He had been at it for a while. The page in front of him held the outlines of two boys, sitting by a pond not unlike this one. The strokes were light, almost unsure. The faces were left unfinished—just the vaguest contours of eyes, a nose, a suggestion of a smile.

Gokul stared at the sketch, biting the inside of his cheek.

He was waiting.

Then came the familiar sound of soft, almost bouncing footsteps. And the unmistakable voice that followed.

"Entha Picasso, finished your masterpiece?"

Gokul looked up to see Taher standing there, slightly breathless, a sheepish grin spread wide on his face. He was in his usual—loose T-shirt, black trackpants, and his hair was still a little damp, curling at the ends.

"Where were you?" Gokul asked, mock annoyed. "We had a morning adventure pact."

Taher chuckled. "Nature had its own adventure plan for me. Took a bit longer."

"Stomach still upset?" Gokul raised an eyebrow.

"Fine now," Taher waved it off, sitting beside him with a dramatic plop. "It's all peaceful inside. Like your sketchbook, apparently."

Before Gokul could cover the page, Taher's eyes had already caught a glimpse.

"What are you drawing?" he asked, his voice softening.

"It's nothing," Gokul said quickly, closing the book.

Taher leaned in with that quiet insistence only he could pull off. "Come on... show me?"

Gokul hesitated. The breeze blew a few strands of hair across his forehead. He pushed them back and finally spoke.

"Okay. But only if you walk with me," he said, standing up and dusting his pants. "There's something I've been meaning to tell you. Been carrying it for too long."

Taher blinked, stood up without a word, and followed.

They began walking along the path that curved beside the stream—its banks lined with wild grass, dragonflies darting between the reeds, and the distant sound of a temple bell somewhere far off.

"It's not school," Gokul started, his voice low. "I mean, everyone thought it was just the board exam stress. But it wasn't."

Taher didn't speak. He knew when not to.

"It's Jobin," Gokul continued, his fingers gripping the sketchbook tighter. "My best friend. We were... always together. Like, people thought we were inseparable. We used to joke that even our attendance got marked together."

Taher smiled faintly.

"But something changed," Gokul said, stopping to pluck a blade of grass and twirl it between his fingers. "And I don't know when exactly. Or why. He started avoiding me. First, small things—like skipping our lunch breaks.

Then it got worse. He stopped replying. Ghosted me completely."

He paused, staring at the stream, as if the answers might be hiding between the ripples.

"Do you think he found out something?" Gokul thought for himself, not looking at Taher. "Something about me. Something I didn't even know how to say out loud back then?"

The silence wasn't heavy. It was just... real.

They kept walking.

Gokul didn't say more. Not yet. Some stories had to unravel slowly, like old yarn being teased out of a tight ball.

But for now, at least, the words had begun to flow.

***

Flashback: Kochi

The sky over Kochi was a soft blue that afternoon, speckled with slow-moving clouds, as if even the city was in no rush. Gokul stood by the window, his hands folded, staring into nothing. His mind, however, was set–**it was Jobin's birthday tomorrow.**

And this time, he had a plan.

Jobin had once said, in one of their long evening walks back from school, that if he could ever own anything absolutely wild, it would be a **WWE championship belt**—like the one Roman Reigns used to flash around. He'd said it laughing, brushing it off, but Gokul had noticed the glint in his eyes.

So that morning, Gokul checked his wallet, carefully counting coins and folded ten-rupee notes. A total of ₹267. Enough.

He jumped on his cycle, ignoring the afternoon heat pressing against his skin, and pedaled hard to the nearest crafts store. There, he picked up **black chart paper, gold foil stickers, glitter pens**, and **red and silver tapes**. Then he rode to the hardware shop—where he asked the shop uncle if he had any scrap cardboard lying around. Uncle handed him a piece, amused. "School project?" he asked.

Gokul nodded, "Something like that."

By the time he reached home, the sun had dipped lower. He called out a quick **"Hi, Amma!"** as he rushed in, dodging the sofa in the hallway.

Latha barely caught a glimpse of him before he vanished into his room, shutting the door behind.

And then—**the mission began**.

Scissors snipped. Tape crackled. The chart paper curled like it had a mind of its own. Gokul worked with a strange calm intensity, the way he always did when it came to Jobin. He carefully cut the cardboard into shape, layering the base with sleek black paper. He used the gold foil for the centre plate—he even etched "WORLD HEAVYWEIGHT CHAMPION" across it.. The side plates? Old metal badges from a school bag, glued with precision.

Finally, he added a glossy red sticker along the edges for a final touch.

As he glued on the last buckle—cut from an old belt—he sat back and admired it.

The WWE championship belt. Handmade. Scrap to sparkle.

It wasn't perfect—but in the way only something made with love could be, Gokul had pulled off a brilliant DIY championship belt.

Because it was for Jobin.

He laid it on the bed like a treasure. His heart thudded softly.

A small smile broke on his face as he whispered, "He's going to love this."

***

The next morning buzzed with a different kind of energy. Gokul had packed the belt inside a plastic bag, its corners jutting out awkwardly. He had to take out two notebooks from his bag just to make space. *"Worth it,"* he thought, locking the bag with a grin.

As he cycled to school, the morning breeze fluttered through his unkempt hair. He kept imagining Jobin's face—surprised, amused, and then melting into that full, crooked smile.

When he reached the class, Jobin was already there—leaning against the window, half-lost in the physics book, his school tie already halfway loosened. Gokul's heart did a little jump. He rushed to him, hugged him from the side.

"Happy birthday, idiot!" he said, cheeky.

Jobin looked up, smiling. He smelt of his usual strong perfume—sharp, citrusy—with that underlying sweet, unmistakable scent of his skin. Gokul couldn't name it, but it always lingered. It stayed on his mind like an unfinished song.

"You didn't forget," Jobin beamed.

"Forget your birthday? Not in this lifetime," Gokul chuckled. "Now close your eyes."

Jobin blinked. "Why?"

"Just close them, please."

With a sigh and a playful eye roll, Jobin closed his eyes. The classroom was beginning to fill, a few of their classmates now watching.

Gokul unzipped his bag with shaky hands, pulled out the belt, and quietly walked behind Jobin. With a dramatic sweep, he wrapped it around Jobin's waist and fastened it.

"Presenting to you... the reigning WWE World Champion–Jobin Mathew!" Gokul declared.

The class erupted with laughter and claps. "Whoa!" someone shouted. "That's so cool!"

Jobin opened his eyes–and for a moment, he just stared. "Dude... what–did you make this?"

Gokul nodded, suddenly shy. "Cardboard, tape, a couple of stickers. Don't judge the glue job."

Jobin's eyes lit up. "This is... this is amazing." And then, without warning, he pulled Gokul in and hugged him tight. His arms were soft but firm, and before pulling back, Jobin placed a quick kiss on Gokul's cheek.

Gokul froze. And then... he laughed–loud, bashful, red-cheeked laughter.

"This is the best gift I've ever got. Seriously. Ever," Jobin said, his voice cracking slightly from excitement.

Gokul smiled, touched his own cheek without thinking. The warmth still lingered there, just like the perfume.

"Happy birthday, champ," he said quietly.

***

Gokul didn't notice when he stopped speaking. His eyes were glued to the flowing stream, but his mind was still far behind—caught in a classroom, a birthday, the scent of old memories. The silence between them had stretched too long.

Taher gently nudged him.

"You've been staring for a while," he said, a soft smile playing on his lips, concern tucked beneath his tone.

Gokul blinked. "Hmm?"

Taher placed his hand on Gokul's shoulder and leaned in slightly, grounding him. "It's okay," he said, voice low and certain. His palm warm and steady, like a friend holding you steady in a storm. "Some people drift away... and sometimes, for no reason at all."

There was something in the way he said it. His voice changed—just a small shift, like a note breaking in a song. "It's the age, no? We're all trying to rediscover who we are. In that journey, we lose some people... and gain new ones."

He paused and let the breeze fill the silence.

"True friendships stay. Others drop off, Gokul."

Gokul turned to look at him.

Taher's eyes had that faraway shimmer now, reflecting more than just sunlight. "I had someone too," he continued. "More than a friend. He took care of me, pampered me like I was a baby. Understood me when I couldn't explain myself."

"What happened?" Gokul asked softly.

"Life," Taher replied with a small, sad laugh. "He left for the city after school. Higher studies. Said we'd stay in touch. For a while, we did. Then... the calls became texts. The texts became silence. And now—now he's back in the village sometimes, but he's always *too busy* to meet me. Though I see his photos—him laughing with the others. People change. That's the one thing I've learnt."

Gokul nodded slowly. "You're right. It's a painful truth."

Taher smiled and patted his back, firmly this time. "It's okay to feel sad that Jobin left. It meant something to you—that's why it hurts. But now, you have to accept the change. Let go. You don't know what life holds for you next, Gokul. And sometimes... sometimes you're so busy looking back, you fail to see the gems already in front of you."

There was a pause.

Gokul looked at Taher. Something passed between them. A quiet understanding. A shared ache. He didn't say anything. He just moved forward and pulled Taher into a hug.

Taher smelled the same—like sun-ripened guava, warm and fruity, sweet with something raw underneath. His body felt firmer this time, solid, a contrast to Gokul's soft belly pressing against him. He could feel the definition in Taher's chest, the faint rise and fall of breath.

"I'm glad I came," Gokul whispered, voice barely above the breeze. "Coming here... was the best decision I ever made."

They didn't let go immediately.

***

Dinner was slow and sweet, like most things in the village. Lakshmiamma had made beetroot thoran, chena mezhukkupuratti, and that special tamarind curry Gokul always asked for. Aravind Achachan grumbled about the rasam being too thin, only to slurp it down like it was divine.

After the meal, they all sat together for a while. The news was playing on the TV, low volume, the anchor's voice barely making it past the sound of the crickets outside. Achachan dozed off halfway into a weather report, his snores rising and falling like lazy waves. Gokul sat between them, his hands wrapped around a steel tumbler of warm water, his heart quietly full.

Eventually, they both retired to their room—his grandmother calling out, "Don't stay up late, mone," as she disappeared behind the beaded curtain.

"I won't, ammamma," he smiled, knowing well he might.

He sat there for a few more minutes, letting the silence nestle around him. Then, with a quiet stretch and a yawn, he got up and switched off the TV. The room dimmed. The only light now came from the moon slipping through the half-drawn curtains.

It had been a good day.

A strange thought, but a true one.

Not perfect, not dramatic, not even productive—but it felt like something inside him had unknotted a little. Something light, something easy. It had been a long time since he felt that way about a day... or about himself.

In his room, the sketchbook still lay on the bed, just where he left it.

He picked it up and sat cross-legged for a moment, tracing the lines he'd drawn that morning. Two boys under the gulmohar tree. Their faces still blank, unnamed. But the outline, the air around them, it felt personal.

Gokul rolled over on the bed, resting the sketchbook by the pillow. His eyes lingered on the faint pencil strokes—half story, half secret. He thought about the walk by the stream, about Taher's voice, the gentleness in his eyes, the hug that lingered longer than it needed to.

A pause. Then came a smile.

A soft, sleepy, uncontrollable smile.

And with that, Gokul pulled the blanket over him, let out a slow sigh, and closed his eyes—still smiling.

Chapter 6: The Smell of Summer

The summer heat had started to show its teeth. Even the breeze that crept through the half-open windows carried a certain heaviness now. But this morning, it was different. The air was thick with the sweet, heady aroma of ripe jackfruit—sticky, golden, unmistakable. It wafted through the cracks of Aravind Achachan's house and tugged Gokul gently out of sleep.

Eyes half-shut, hair a bird's nest, he followed the scent like a cartoon character floating behind a pie. There, in the kitchen, ammamma and achachan were deep into the business of jackfruit—fingers sticky, hands glistening, tongues clicking at the stubbornness of each pod. Achachan muttered something about how these were "thenvarikka" and not the bland kind. Ammamma nodded without looking up, her hands expertly prying open the honeycomb-like heart of the fruit.

"Mone da, help with this," she said without looking.

Gokul washed his hands and joined in, picking out the golden bulbs and dropping them into a steel bowl. The thick sap clung to his fingers, gluing them together in syrupy defiance. He licked it off.

Once the fruit was cleaned, Gokul triumphantly took a full plate and dashed off to the drawing room. He plopped onto the diwan, turned on the TV to some morning music on the Malayalam channel, and—because it's second nature by now—snapped a quick pic for his Insta stories. "*Jackfruit Heaven*"

He gulped down the jackfruit one by one, chewing less, tasting more. Sticky fingers, a sugar rush in his chest, and soft Malayalam melodies in the background. It was almost cinematic.

But not for long.

"Look at your hair, mone!" came Laxmiamma's voice from the kitchen door. She clicked her tongue and walked toward him with purpose.

Before Gokul could escape, she was already back with her bottle of coconut oil, that iconic dark brown glass container with a dried curry leaf floating like a charm inside it.

"You want to end up like your Achan? Bald?" she asked, already pouring the warm oil onto his scalp.

"Aiyyo, Laxmiamma!"

"Sit still, da." She started massaging his head like a woman on a mission—circular strokes, tugging and kneading like she was fixing more than just split ends.

Gokul sat there, surrendering. Outside, Aravind Achachan sat in the veranda with his paper, legs crossed, specs resting low on his nose. His hair, though grey, still clung to his scalp with admirable loyalty.

Gokul glanced at him, then chuckled. "Looks like I still have a chance."

After a good oil bath to the head and some teasing banter with Laxmiamma, Gokul felt almost reborn. He looked at the clock. Still early.

A bath in the stream. That thought alone made his spine tingle with excitement. He hadn't touched the river since arriving. Not properly.

Still sitting on the diwan, oil now cooling on his scalp, he opened WhatsApp and typed out a quick message:

Gokul: "Wanna go take a dip in the river?"

Taher: "YES. Coming. Our usual spot?"

Gokul: "Yes."

Gokul smiled, put the phone aside, and stretched his arms like a cat. The stream awaited. And so did something else, maybe.

***

The sun had climbed higher by the time Gokul reached the stream. The earth beneath his feet was warm, the air heavy with the scent of sun-baked grass, wild jasmine, and damp soil. He could hear the soft gurgle of the stream before he could see it. Their usual spot was still untouched–shaded by overhanging bamboo and guarded by the gentle bend of the riverbank. It looked like something out of a dream Gokul used to have, back when everything felt confusing and nothing had a name.

Taher was already there, standing shirtless by the rocks, his mundu hitched up above the knees. He waved when he saw Gokul and called out, "Took you long enough!"

Gokul waved back, but his heart was beating faster than it should. The image before him caught him off-guard–Taher in the golden light, his chest bare, a faint sheen of sweat on his skin, his lean muscles sharp under the sun, and yet... something soft in the way he stood, hand resting on his waist, hip tilted just a little, a curve in the posture that made Gokul's throat dry.

Gokul looked away too quickly and forced a laugh. "Blame Laxmiamma. She poured half a bottle of oil on my head."

Taher grinned. "Good. You need it. Your hair was beginning to look like an abandoned nest."

They chuckled. Then, in silence, they both stripped down to their towels. Gokul turned his back, pretending to fuss with his shirt, but he stole a glance—Taher's back was a painting: scarred slightly from old mosquito bites, tanned, water glistening where he had splashed himself. His waist narrow, towel knotted loosely, dangerously low.

Gokul caught his breath. A rush of warmth swept over him, panic trailing close behind. Something inside him stirred, pressed against his ribs like a question he was too scared to answer.

They slipped into the stream, yelping as the cool water bit at their skin.

"Aiyyo, it's freezing!" Taher gasped.

"You're such a baby," Gokul teased, diving in headfirst. The water was clear, playful, tickling his arms as he swam deeper. The summer sun reflected in shimmers, dancing on the surface.

Taher soon followed, splashing water toward Gokul.

"Not fair!" Gokul laughed, wiping his face. "I didn't do anything!"

"Now you did," Taher grinned, sending another wave toward him.

They swam and splashed and chased each other like schoolboys let out early. Gokul forgot about the world. The only thing that mattered was the laughter echoing off the riverbanks, and the boy beside him.

But it came back. As they stood at the shallow end, catching their breath, Gokul glanced again—Taher was leaning on a rock, half out of the water, droplets tracing down his chest, head tilted back, eyes closed. There was that same softness again. Not just in posture, but in essence. Masculine but tender, hard yet glowing with something gentler. Gokul couldn't look away.

Taher opened his eyes. "What?" he asked, catching Gokul staring.

Gokul blinked, caught. "I was just... I mean... you've grown stronger, da."

"Too much sun," Taher grinned, flexing dramatically.

They laughed, and the tension evaporated, but only for a moment. Gokul turned quickly toward the stream, hoping the water would cool more than just his skin.

They fooled around like boys do—racing across the shallow side, playing splash-fight, dunking each other's heads under. Gokul caught himself watching Taher a little too long—how the water clung to his face, how his hair slicked back, how he smiled with his whole body.

At one point, Gokul leaned back against a rock, catching his breath, chest rising and falling, water droplets gliding down his neck.

"Taher..."

"Hm?"

"There's something I should've said long back. Something about me."

Taher turned to him, eyes soft, curious. "You okay?"

"I... sometimes feel different. Like, I don't know if... I don't know if I'm like the others."

There was a beat of silence. Gokul swallowed. He couldn't say it yet. The words sat like marbles on his tongue.

But Taher just nodded slowly, stepping closer. "Different's not bad, Gokul. Sometimes different is just... the beginning of real."

Gokul looked into his eyes, his breath caught somewhere between fear and relief. Taher stood still, his posture soft—almost delicate—as if something unspoken had brushed past him. There was a flicker of sadness in his gaze, like an old memory had stirred. Then, almost like shaking it off, he ran his fingers through his wet hair, pushing it back from his face with quiet confidence.

"Being different is good, Gokul," Taher said agian, his voice low but steady.

Their eyes held—just for a moment longer than usual. No words, just the hum of the stream and the silence that speaks when two hearts stand a little too close to the truth.

Taher broke the silence by splashing Gokul again. "Come. Last one to that tree is a monkey"

And just like that, the moment dissolved into laughter and splashing and the kind of joy that only happens when two hearts understand more than words.

Later, lying on the sun-warmed rocks to dry off, their wet towels wrapped around their waists, Gokul let his eyes flutter closed, the scent of river water and guava skin still clinging to the air between them.

Whatever this was… it felt real. And for now, that was enough.

***

The sky had turned a deep shade of orange, that burnt-glow kind of evening the village wore so well. After jackfruit, it was now mango season—sweet, golden, sticky summers wrapped in fruit.

Gokul sat cross-legged on the diwan as Aravind Achachan returned from the backyard, holding a small basket of ripe Priyoor mangoes.

"Handpicked just now," he said proudly, showing one that was perfectly sun-kissed, freckled, and slightly splitting at the seam from ripeness.

"You and your timing, Achacha," Gokul laughed, reaching for one.

Aravind Achacha peeled it slowly, cut into slices and put them on a plate.. Gokul eagerly picked the biggest slice first, the juice already dripping down his wrist before the first bite. Sweet, fleshy, and almost floral—like eating the sun itself.

"Eat slowly, or you'll get a throat ache," Lakshmiamma called out from inside, as if on cue.

Gokul smiled, stuffed another slice in his mouth, then got up with a plate full of sliced mangoes and quietly made his way to the backyard. Past the tulsi pot, over the gravel path, and down to the banks of the stream. The air was warm but calming, the breeze smelled of water and wildflowers.

He sat on the edge, legs stretched, the mango plate resting beside him. The stream shimmered, mirroring the last light of day.

But his mind—his mind wasn't here.

It was back in the water. Back to the earlier hours, when the current was soft, and Taher's laughter had echoed across the ripples.

That moment—just them, towels clinging to damp skin, droplets running down collarbones, closeness thick like humidity.

Gokul bit into a slice of mango, but the taste was muted now.

It wasn't the fruit causing butterflies in his belly.

It was Taher.

The way he moved—graceful, but grounded. The curve of his smile, his soft voice over a strong jaw. The scent of him—sweet like guava warmed under the sun.

Gokul stared into the stream, unsure where the water ended and his thoughts began.

"What is happening?" he murmured aloud.

He wiped his hand, licked the mango juice off his thumb, and closed his eyes for a second.

This feeling... it wasn't new.

A familiar flutter stirred within.

He remembered.

Jobin.

His face shifted. A little tension around the mouth, a little stiffness in the shoulders.

Back in Kochi, in school—he had felt this before. That strange storm of affection and ache. It wasn't just friendship. He had told himself it was. But he knew better now.

Jobin was more than a friend.

He had meant more.

And for a while, Gokul thought Jobin felt the same. The smiles. The hugs. That kiss on the cheek during the birthday surprise.

But then... he didn't.

The silence. The drifting. The cold absence.

Gokul's breath hitched a little.

He picked up another slice, held it mid-air for a second, then put it back down.

He wasn't hungry anymore.

Chapter 7: The Beginning of a Pause

Lunch break was usually their time.

The corridors buzzed with the clatter of tiffin boxes, steel spoons, and laughter echoing off worn-out walls of the higher secondary block. The mango tree outside the canteen cast a long shadow over the dusty courtyard, where students huddled in familiar groups, their ties loosened, and their guards too.

Gokul had finished his lunch. He walked to the wash area with his steel box. The cold water slapped his face awake as he washed his mouth, eyes still scanning around.

"Where is he?" he muttered to himself, flicking water off his fingers.

Jobin usually waited. Always did.

They had their rhythm – eat together, laugh together, walk the corridor together like a scene from a buddy film. Gokul turned toward their usual hangout spot behind the chemistry lab. Empty.

"Strange," Gokul whispered, clutching the tiffin box tighter.

A sudden laugh caught his ear. That familiar high-pitched giggle. He turned quickly and saw him.

Jobin – standing under the steps that led to the auditorium, surrounded by a group of boys from the commerce batch. Giggling. Hands flying in animated stories. Their ties hung loose, one of them mimicking a teacher's walk. Everyone cracked up.

Jobin too. His shoulders bounced, his smile wide.

Gokul felt a twitch in his chest.

A slow, silent pang.

That smile... he hadn't seen it directed at him in a while.

With an impulsive stride, Gokul walked over, trying not to show he was breathless.

"Hey," he said, forcing a grin as he nudged into the group.

The conversation paused for a second, some heads turned. One of them—Midhun, gave him a half-smile, the kind that doesn't really reach the eyes.

"Yo Gokul," Jobin said, not meeting his eyes properly, already glancing elsewhere.

"What's going on?" Gokul asked, trying to blend into the half-heard joke.

"Oh, just some dumb stuff about Kiran Sir's hair gel addiction," Jobin laughed, and everyone picked the joke back up.

Gokul chuckled half-heartedly, trying to catch up, trying to belong. The laughter sounded hollow now, like he had walked in too late into a room where the warmth had already left.

He stood there, nodding, letting words fly past him. He didn't know what stung more – the fact that Jobin didn't make space for him in the group, or the fact that Jobin didn't even notice he hadn't.

Suddenly, the bell rang – short and sharp. The clanging sound snapped the courtyard back into order.

The boys disbanded in seconds, like water spilt on sun-baked tiles. One by one,they trotted back into their respective classes.

Jobin too.

No glance back.

No "Let's go."

No waiting.

Gokul stood still for a moment, eyes fixed at the spot where Jobin had stood seconds ago.

Something had shifted.

He couldn't name it, but he could feel it – thick like humidity, heavy like clouds before a storm.

***

The sun was lower now, casting long shadows on the pond. The stone steps were warm under Gokul's bare feet as he sat by the pond, legs pulled up, flicking small pebbles into the lazy water. *Plop... plop...* The ripples spread out like his thoughts – widening, deepening, fading.

A pebble in his hand hovered a second too long before he tossed it in.

Before his mind could dive too far into the spiral of *Jobin* and everything unresolved, a familiar voice floated in:

"Sorry I'm late..."

Gokul looked up – there he was. Taher, in his usual maroon tee and faded trackpants, grinning that sheepish grin, brushing a loose curl behind his ear.

"What took you so long? I WhatsApped you an hour ago." Gokul tried to sound stern, but the smile on his face betrayed him.

"Toilet emergency," Taher said with a laugh and plopped down beside him. The scent hit Gokul again – guava, sun-dried and sweet, and now he realised – addictive. His body almost responded before his mind could register.

"Started sketching your designs yet?" Gokul asked, masking the flutter inside.

Taher nodded, leaning back on his elbows. "Yeah, a little bit. Will show you once I have a handful, okay?"

"I'm holding you to that," Gokul smirked.

They both looked out at the shimmering pond for a while, the quiet between them comfortable. Birds cawed in the distance, someone's cow bell clinked softly.

"Temple festival's tomorrow," Gokul said casually. "Coming with me?"

Taher tilted his head. "Hmm. My folks won't really be happy about it... but I'll come. For you."

Something flickered inside Gokul. He quickly picked another stone and flicked it away.

After a small pause, Taher spoke, his voice softer this time. "Still thinking about *him*, aren't you? You need closure, Gokul."

Gokul felt the words land hard. He exhaled sharply. "Let's not go there today." He forced a smile. "Let's go to Balan Chettan's kada. I got some money. His uzhunu vada... nothing beats that after Ammama's pazhampori."

Taher laughed. "Done."

A few minutes later, Taher's cycle rattled onto the path. Gokul hopped up, dusted his shorts, and as always, perched himself on the front rail. The ride began – familiar, comforting. The breeze, the slight bumps on the road, and that scent again... guava in the sun, earthy and sweet.

Gokul held onto the handlebar, leaning back slightly. *How can someone's presence feel this warm?* he wondered.

Balan Chettan's kada was buzzing with the usual crowd – old men sipping tea, a few school kids sharing a plate of pazham pori, women packing parcels.

"Two uzhunu vada, two parippu vada, two chai," Gokul called out.

As they waited, he nudged Taher playfully. "Your uzhunu vada's mine if you take too long."

True to his word, when the steaming plate arrived, Gokul promptly stole a bite from Taher's vada, grinning wide.

"You moron!" Taher laughed, swatting his arm.

Just then, Balan Chettan came over. “Aren’t you Suresh’s son? Haven’t seen you in a while.”

“Yes, Chetta,” Gokul smiled politely. “Here for the holidays. Missed your vadas.”

“Good, good. Tell your achan that I asked.” With a grin, Balan Chettan shuffled away.

The boys munched in comfortable silence, the sounds of life around them grounding everything.

Later, the sun dipped lower as they cycled back. This time, Gokul sat quieter, taking it all in.

Outside his house, Taher stopped. They both lingered.

“It’s nice... being around you,” Gokul said softly, looking into Taher’s eyes. “Thanks for spending these days with me.”

Taher’s eyes glistened. A tear escaped before he could wipe it. With a half-smile, voice thick, he whispered, “What else am I for, idiot Gokul...”

Gokul smiled, warmth blooming in his chest. No more words needed.

Chapter 8:
The Night of Lights

The sun had barely dipped below the paddy fields when the temple ground buzzed to life. Strings of fairy lights blinked lazily across the arches. The air smelled of jasmine, camphor, roasted peanuts, and something more – *memories.*

Gokul made his way to the temple with Ammama and Achachan, weaving through groups of relatives and unfamiliar aunties who grabbed his cheeks like he was still ten.

"Aiyyo, Sureshettan's son, isn't it? How big you've become!"

"And thin also! Does your mother feed you or not?"

Gokul smiled politely, nodded, made a few polite bows, and tried not to roll his eyes. His mind was elsewhere – scanning the crowd, looking... until–

"Da!"

There he was. Taher, standing by a lamp post, eyes catching his instantly.

Gokul turned to Ammama, whispered, "Im joining Taher. I can't handle the peskering aunties no more"

"Go, go... careful, ah!" she said, waving him off with a smile.

In a few quick steps, Gokul was beside Taher. Both of them wore crisp mundus and shirts. Gokul was still trying to master the art of walking without tripping on the cloth.

"This is impossible," Gokul mumbled, tugging at the edge of his mundu. "I swear I'll flash the whole crowd at this rate."

Taher chuckled, eyes gleaming. "Come here."

Before Gokul could protest, Taher moved closer, arms around Gokul's waist, fingers deftly folding and knotting the mundu tighter. Gokul stood frozen, heart hammering as Taher's fingers brushed his soft skin, knuckles grazing the curve of his belly.

"There... you'll survive the night," Taher whispered, voice warm against his ear.

Gokul swallowed hard. "Thanks... I think," he muttered, eyes flicking away to hide the blush rising in his cheeks.

They strolled past the festive stalls, shoulder to shoulder, bumping lightly now and then.

"Ooh, look," Taher pointed. "That chain is nice."

Without hesitation, he picked a thin chain with a tiny black pendant and a bracelet that leaned more towards a bangle in design.

"Aw, that's gonna look good on your wrist" Gokul teased.

Taher smiled, eyes soft.

Gokul grinned, heart swelling. He picked a few quirky rings – one black, one with a fake ruby, and slipped them on.

They laughed, bantered, watched the devotees light rows of lamps, the priests move in sync with the temple drums.

But soon Gokul noticed Taher shifting – shoulders hunched, breaths shallower. The crowd pressing in, loud chants echoing.

"Taher..." Gokul whispered. "Come."

He led him away, past the main stalls, around the corner to a quieter patch near the back temple wall, where only the hum of the festivities remained in the air.

Without a word, Gokul wrapped his arms around Taher, holding him tight.

"Shhh... just breathe."

Taher's body was tense, but slowly – breath by breath – Gokul felt him soften in his arms, his strong frame melting into Gokul's softer one.

Heartbeats – Gokul could hear Taher's racing. His scent was intoxicating now – sun-ripened guava, musk, and something tender, *aching*.

For a moment, Gokul held on longer than he should've. His own pulse wild, cheeks warm.

Finally, breaking the silence, he whispered, "Feeling better now, da?"

A small nod. "Yes. And... sorry, Gokul... for spoiling the mood."

Gokul smiled softly, pulling back just enough to look into those pale, kind eyes.

"What else am I for, idiot Taher?" he echoed, voice gentle.

A slow smile bloomed on Taher's face, eyes shimmering with something unspoken.

They walked back slowly, fingers brushing until they laced naturally – a quiet, perfect fit. Hand in hand, they stood at the edge of the temple grounds, watching the festival unfold from a slight distance.

The drums reached a fever pitch, the crowd roared, and the first crackle of fireworks lit up the night sky.

Boom – red.

Boom – green.

Boom – gold.

Gokul squeezed Taher's hand tighter as the colours rained above them.

Neither spoke.

Neither needed to.

The night had already told them more than words could.

***

Next Morning

The sun was already slipping in bold and bright through the old wooden windows when Gokul stirred. The room was warm, lit in soft gold.

He stretched lazily, limbs sprawling across the old cotton bed, the pillow warm from the night's sleep. His mind, though, was already running ahead – *last night.*

The fireworks.

Taher's fingers laced with his.

That moment under the rain of colours, where words had melted away.

A small smile tugged at Gokul's lips. He exhaled slowly, heart blooming again.

Dragging himself upright, he pulled on a loose t-shirt and padded out of the room, still a little sleepy-eyed. It was already past ten.

In the hall, Lakshmiamma sat watching TV – a loud morning serial where two heavily made-up women were arguing about something grave.

"Good morning, Ammama," Gokul greeted, voice still thick with sleep.

Lakshmiamma turned, eyes softening instantly.

"Good morning, mone! You finally woke up. Slept well?"

Gokul smiled, running a hand through his messy hair.

"Hmm... very well," he said, thinking again of the night under stars.

"In that case," she grinned, "go brush your teeth first."

Gokul chuckled. "Ammamaaa... what's for breakfast?"

She switched off the TV volume a bit, leaning back.

"Masala dosa today. With chutney and sambhar. Your favourite, no?"

His face lit up. "Oh wow! Now I'm definitely brushing fast."

Lakshmiamma laughed. "Go, go... Achachan is also waiting."

Through the open door to the veranda, Gokul spotted Aravind Achachan, lying on his reclining chair, half asleep, newspaper draped across his chest.

"Good morning, Achacha!" Gokul called out.

Achachan stirred, eyes cracking open.

"Good morning, Gokula. Had a good time at the festival, ah?" he asked, voice gravelly from sleep.

Gokul smiled, memories flashing again.

"Yes, Achacha. It was beautiful."

"Hmm... now go eat well. You've gotten thinner these days," Achachan muttered, closing his eyes again.

Grinning, Gokul padded off to brush and freshen up, stomach already growling in anticipation of crisp dosa and chutney waiting on the table.

Today felt like another good day ahead.

***

The afternoon sun had settled into a sleepy golden haze over the temple ground. The final rites of the festival had begun. The crowd had thickened – a wave of colorful shirts, sarees, and the low, booming rhythm of *chenda melam* weaving its way through the air like thunder rolling in.

Gokul stood by the fence, his phone in hand. The temple elephant, majestic and calm, stood still as a rock with the deity perched proudly atop, its trunk draped in the glittering *nettipattom*, bells clinking softly with every slight sway. The scent of incense, oil, and ripe bananas lingered everywhere.

He panned his camera slowly, catching the rhythm of the drums, the crowd swaying, and the flickering heat.

One boomerang. Two slow-motion reels. He added them to his stories with the caption:

"Ending the Ulsavam with a little more rhythm and grace."

"Late again," Gokul said without looking, feeling the familiar warmth beside him.

Taher grinned, a little out of breath, hair tousled. "Fashionably."

They took a few selfies – one serious, one goofy, one with the elephant blurred in the background. Gokul posted them with a sticker that said *"Festive Day Feels."*

"Come," Taher said, pulling at Gokul's arm. "Let's look at the stalls."

The stalls were lined with chaos – bright dupattas, sequined tops, cheap perfumes, fake Ray-Bans, and rubbery sandals. They laughed at a tee that said "Adidos" and stopped by a stall selling earrings shaped like fish.

"I'd totally wear these if I had a piercing," Gokul mused, holding one up to his ear.

"I dare you to," Taher smirked.

They moved on and found a small corner where a man was frying *bajji* – the smell of gram flour, chili, and sweat thick in the air. They got a plate of *chilli bajji* each and leaned against the makeshift stall counter.

Just as Gokul took a big bite, he noticed Taher freeze mid-chew.

Following his gaze, Gokul turned.

Standing across the dusty path was a boy with a girl beside him, her hand looped lightly through his. He looked leaner now, hair shorter, eyes still unreadable.

"Is that...?" Gokul asked softly.

Taher nodded. "Subin."

The name hung heavy.

"You okay?" Gokul asked, wiping his fingers and gently placing a hand on Taher's arm.

"I don't know," Taher whispered. "It's weird. I didn't expect to see him here. Or with her."

"Let's go," Gokul said, suddenly firm. "Let's talk to him. Get a closure, maybe?"

"I don't–"

"You don't have to say anything deep. Just let him know you're good. That you've moved on. And that you're... better."

He took Taher's hand. "Come."

They walked toward Subin, who noticed them midway and stiffened slightly. But he managed a smile.

"Hey! Taher! It's been... long."

"Yeah," Taher said, voice calm, almost blank. "It has."

Subin's eyes flicked to Gokul, then to the girl beside him. She looked politely curious.

"I'm Gokul," Gokul offered, flashing a half-smile.

"Nice to meet you," the girl said quietly.

Taher took a moment, then said, "Life's been good, actually. Lot better these days."

Subin nodded slowly, unsure. "Glad to hear that."

Taher gave a small smile, too brief to be read. "Anyway... we're just heading off. Got a lot left to see."

And just like that, he turned, Gokul following beside him.

As they walked away, Taher didn't speak for a while. They stopped at a stall with cloth handbags, but neither of them looked at the items.

"How do you feel?" Gokul finally asked.

Taher let out a shaky breath. "Like I finally took something off my chest."

Gokul gave him a gentle pat on the back. "That's it. Now just try to be in peace with it."

Taher nodded. “He felt like a ghost until today. Now... he’s just a stranger.”

They turned away from the bustle of the festival, walking through the thinning crowd as the last rhythms of the *chenda* echoed in the distance.

“Where to now?” Taher asked, voice lighter.

“Our spot?” Gokul said, already smiling.

They walked the narrow path to the pond. The festival behind them. The quiet ahead.

As the sun began its descent again, they sat near the water, legs stretched out, soft wind brushing their faces.

For a while, they didn’t speak.

They just... breathed.

Together.

***

The pond lay still, almost mirror-like, save for the gentle ripples that danced with the breeze. The golden hour was stretching across the sky, blushing everything it touched. Birds called out in the distance, the scent of dry earth and fading incense drifting faintly from the temple grounds far behind them.

Gokul sat with his knees drawn up, arms hugging them lightly. His chin rested on his forearm. Taher lay flat on the grass, one arm behind his head, the other drawing lazy circles in the air.

Neither spoke for a long while.

Gokul reached for a small twig beside him and began doodling on the mud. Lines, loops, two faceless boys. He stopped midway and glanced sideways.

"Tired?" he asked softly.

"Mmhmm," Taher hummed. "But in a good way. Like... emptied."

Gokul smiled faintly. "Yeah. Me too."

A few dragonflies buzzed past them. Somewhere, a distant motorbike hummed and faded. Time slowed.

"You know what I like about this pond?" Gokul said, almost whispering.

"What?"

"It doesn't ask questions. Doesn't want explanations. You can just... come here and exist."

Taher turned to his side, propped up on one elbow, looking at him. "Like you."

Gokul turned, caught off guard. "Huh?"

"You don't ask too many questions either. You just let me be," Taher said. His eyes lingered a moment too long.

The silence between them deepened.

Gokul felt a tingle down his spine – not fear, not discomfort. Just awareness. Of being seen. Of being held, even without touch.

He chuckled, trying to break the weight. “Well, I do have questions. I just save them for later.”

Taher laughed, sitting up now, brushing grass off his shirt. “Shoot.”

Gokul looked down at the twig in his hand, then at the fading sketch on the earth. “Why did Subin stop talking to you?”

The air shifted.

Taher exhaled through his nose. “Because I was... too much, I think. Too close. Too soft. Too emotional. Too... me.”

Gokul blinked. “That doesn’t sound like a bad thing.”

Taher smiled, not bitterly, but like someone who’d learned to live with the ache. “Sometimes, it is. Especially when you don't fit into their idea of how boys should be.”

Gokul looked at him, really looked. His wet lashes from earlier, his slightly cracked lips from sun and wind, his posture always a little curved, like he was apologizing for taking up space.

“I think you’re just enough,” Gokul whispered.

Taher looked at him – not surprised, but something softer. "So are you."

Their eyes lingered, the pond reflecting flecks of gold and stillness around them. Then, Taher sighed and shifted, pulling his legs out of the water and hugging his knees close.

"Anyway," he said gently, brushing a damp curl from his forehead, "I think I got the closure I needed... finally."

He looked out at the water, voice steady but careful.

Gokul nodded slowly, unsure if he was supposed to say something. He could feel something coming.

Taher turned, meeting Gokul's gaze again. "Don't you... need that too? With Jobin?"

The name landed like a soft thud between them.

Gokul blinked, heart suddenly louder in his chest. He looked down at the water, now still again, as if waiting for a reply too.

"I don't know," he muttered. "I keep thinking I do. Then I tell myself I don't. And then... I see you, and I forget he ever existed. And then I feel guilty for forgetting."

Taher's brows furrowed softly, not out of anger – but understanding.

"You're not forgetting him," Taher said. "You're just... letting the memory fade to where it belongs."

Gokul let that sit for a moment. He picked up a pebble and gently tossed it into the pond. Ripples spread out, clear and quiet.

“I loved him, you know,” Gokul said, almost to himself.

“I know,” Taher whispered.

“And I think... he didn’t know what to do with that love. Maybe it scared him. Or maybe I did.”

“Maybe,” Taher nodded. “Or maybe he was never meant to hold something as soft as you.”

Gokul turned to him again, surprised at the tenderness in his voice. “You really think I’m soft?”

Taher smiled, that lopsided grin of his. “Like summer mangoes left out in the sun too long.”

They laughed – quiet but honest.

“I don't think I’ll ever get the kind of closure you're talking about,” Gokul said after a moment.

“Maybe not,” Taher said. “But maybe you’ll write it. Or sketch it. Or let it go bit by bit, like old pond water draining through cracks.”

The sun was almost gone now, the last streaks of orange melting into blue.

Gokul leaned back on his elbows, sighing deeply. “Why do you always say the right things?”

Taher shrugged. “Maybe because I mean them.”

Silence again. This time it felt different. Not heavy, not awkward. Just... safe.

Then Taher added, "And if you ever want to write that closure... maybe I can be your first reader."

Gokul looked at him, eyes soft and shining.

Taher just leaned gently against Gokul's shoulder – a quiet reminder that not everything soft needs to be broken.

Chapter 9:
The Unsung Love

The fan above Gokul's head whirred lazily, slicing through the sticky afternoon heat. He sat slouched on his wooden bench, the edge of his notebook pressed against his palm, pages filled halfway with hurried notes and halfway with idle scribbles – doodles of half-drawn boys and tangled lines, nothing in particular, everything all at once.

Subin and Vimal were bantering beside him – something about the upcoming sports day or maybe the new chemistry teacher who said "actually" every five seconds. Gokul nodded when expected, laughed in the right places, but his mind had already stepped outside the classroom.

There he was – Jobin. Leaning against the corridor railing, talking animatedly with a few boys from the commerce batch. His laughter echoed faintly through the open window. That sound used to belong to Gokul. That smile. That sparkle in his eyes. Gokul felt it in his stomach – that dull pull of absence.

"Hey, da... what's wrong with you?" Vimal nudged him, glancing over. "You look like you're in heart break."

Gokul gave a weak smile, "Nothing, just sleepy," he muttered, even though he hadn't slept properly in days.

His eyes stayed glued to Jobin.

Ever since Jobin started drifting, everything else had gone dull – the textbooks, the class tests, the world itself. Gokul failed his last bio test, not because he didn't know the answers, but because his heart wasn't in it. His heart had taken residency in another boy's pocket. One that didn't check in anymore.

Vimal returned to his chatter with Subin, and Gokul slowly closed his notebook. The weight of the pen in his hand suddenly felt like a burden. Without saying a word, he stood up and walked toward the door.

Jobin was still there – arms crossed, one foot against the wall, laughing at something someone said. Gokul stepped into their circle casually, like he belonged. Like nothing had changed.

"Hey Jobin," he said, his voice light but betraying a crack somewhere deep inside.

Jobin turned to him, the smile dimming just a notch. "Hey da, what's up?"

Gokul caught the scent first – that familiar mix of talcum, ink and a dash of cologne Jobin once said he stole from his dad. Gokul wanted to lean in, to let his head rest on that shoulder just for a second, but he didn't. He stood firm, hands clenched inside his pockets.

"Nothing much," Gokul said, eyes flicking across the group of unfamiliar faces. "I felt boring, so I just stepped out for some air."

One of the commerce boys – tall, annoyingly confident, hair gelled to perfection – smirked. "Welcome to the cool corridor, bro. This is where all the real education happens."

The others chuckled. Jobin laughed too – that same full-throated laugh that used to be Gokul's favorite sound.

Gokul forced a grin, his lips curving upward while something inside him quietly sank.

He lingered there, hovering at the edge of the conversation. He didn't know their inside jokes, their slang, their rhythm. He tried to blend in, to stitch himself into the scene – but it felt like forcing a puzzle piece where it didn't belong anymore.

Jobin didn't look at him the way he used to. His eyes darted across the group, occasionally landing on Gokul like a passing memory – warm, but fading.

"So... you joining for the English elocution thing?" Gokul asked Jobin suddenly, trying to find some common ground.

Jobin shrugged. "Don't think so. Too much work da. Anyway, these guys are planning a music jam that day."

"Oh," Gokul nodded, swallowing the tiny pit in his throat.

The group chuckled at something else and Gokul smiled along, pretending. His fingers itched to touch Jobin's arm. Just once. Just to see if it still sparked.

But he didn't.

Instead, he stood there a little longer, letting the silence stretch between words that should have come. His heart pressed against his chest, wanting to scream: **Look at me. Talk to me like before. Come back to me.**

But all that came out was a tight-lipped smile.

***

The school bus rattled along its usual winding route, the late sun falling in golden streaks through dusty windows. Gokul sat by the window, Jobin next to him – like always. Or at least, how it used to be.

This ride used to be Gokul's favorite part of the day. Just the two of them, squeezed into a two-seater, laughing at stupid jokes or sharing earphones to listen to the same playlist for the hundredth time. But now it was mostly Jobin talking about his new friends from the commerce batch – how funny they were, how they planned to start a YouTube channel, how someone's prank went viral in their group chat.

Gokul smiled where he had to. Nodded where he was expected to. But his eyes stayed out the window, watching trees blur past.

He wanted to ask, *Do you miss me, ever?*

But instead, he faked a yawn and rested his head gently on Jobin's shoulder. It was a little sweaty – a mix of school day heat, faint cologne, and something that was just Jobin. Familiar and intoxicating.

Jobin didn't flinch. In fact, he adjusted a bit, letting Gokul rest better. That small movement, that tiny act of care, sent a warm flutter through Gokul's chest. His breath slowed. His heart calmed.

For a second, just a second, it felt like the old Jobin was still there.

But moments are fragile.

The bus came to a halt at Jobin's stop. Gokul straightened up, rubbing his eyes like he had really been asleep. Jobin stood up, slung his bag over his shoulder and looked back.

"Bye da," Gokul said, trying to make it sound casual.

Jobin smiled and raised his hand, waving – the way he always used to. That small, familiar gesture curved a soft smile onto Gokul's face, one that stayed even as the bus pulled away and Jobin disappeared behind the trees.

Even in heartbreak, some habits refused to fade.

***

That evening felt longer than most.

The TV blared from the living room – the usual news bulletin, loud and hurried. Gokul sat at the dining table with his plate in front of him, the rice steaming gently, sambar spreading into the corners like an unwanted guest. He stirred it absently with his fingers more than he ate. His mother, Latha, sat across him, watching in quiet concern.

"You're barely eating these days," she said softly, scooping more rice onto his plate without waiting for a reply. "Whatever it is, school pressure or something else, don't starve yourself, mone. Replenish the energy."

Gokul nodded, without words. He ate – mechanically, without tasting. A mouthful at a time, as if it were a duty. And then, quietly, he stood up, placed his plate in the sink, and walked up the stairs. Past his father, Suresh, who didn't notice anything except the headline scrolling across the TV.

Upstairs, in the dim yellow light of his desk lamp, Gokul opened a textbook. A random page. Something about photosynthesis. It could've been in Greek.

He stared. Then blinked. Then flipped to the back cover where his old doodles lived. That's when he saw it.

FLAMES.

Gokul + Jobin.

Friendship – Love – Affection – Marriage – Enemies – Sister.

Drawn in messy blue pen, circled with hearts and stars. Silly. Childish. But still there.

A faint smile crept onto Gokul's lips. He traced his finger over the faded ink. He looked up at the ceiling fan whirring lazily, his thoughts tangled in memory.

Was Jobin just a friend? Was this all just longing for someone close?

He stood up restlessly, walked around the room once, twice. Then crashed onto his bed, throwing off his T-shirt like it was too heavy to wear. He lay on his back, staring at the cracks in the ceiling – his arm flung across his forehead.

His cheek still remembered the warmth of Jobin's shoulder. That scent – a mix of school sweat, cologne, and sunshine – still clung to his skin. He didn't want to shower. He didn't want it to leave.

Then, it hit him.

He was in love with Jobin.

Not just the way friends love. Not a crush that would fade in the heat of exams or distance. This was deep. Silent. Soaked into every part of him.

He remembered how he had brushed off Aswathy's advances last semester. How nothing ever clicked with anyone else. Because, all this time, **he was already in love.** He just didn't have the words. Or the courage.

A tear broke loose from the corner of his eye, sliding down to his pillow. He didn't wipe it.

He loved Jobin.

And he had lost him.

Not just a friend. But the boy he wanted to be with for the rest of his life.

And for the first time, he didn't feel shame. Or fear.

Just clarity. Like a fog finally lifting.

This is who he was. This is what it meant to be Gokul.

He liked boys. He loved a boy. And that was okay.

He closed his eyes. His breath slowed. His heart, though heavy, was no longer confused.

Gokul had come to terms with his truth – not because he had planned to, but because love, even when it aches, always leaves behind a kind of light.

Chapter 10: The Weight of Unspoken Words

The lunch plate shimmered in the light slanting through the old wooden windows, warm and dappled. Gokul sat at the dining table, slowly mixing the last bit of sambar with the jackfruit thoran and a little chicken curry – the flavours soaking into each other, just the way Lakshmiamma always said it should be. Next to him, Aravind Achachan ate with practiced ease, his fingers scooping the rice with the same rhythm he'd probably followed for decades.

Lakshmiamma sat besides them, a towel draped over her lap. She never ate with them – she waited, always, until the last plate was washed. Instead, she sat there like the quiet sun of the house, watching, making sure they were fed.

Achachan was mumbling about the neighbour's well running dry. Something about the roadwork damaging the pipelines again. The usual panchayat gossip, peppered with a few grumbles about the ward member who never came.

But Gokul wasn't there – not really.

His hand stirred the food without attention. His eyes watched his plate, but his mind was far.

Jobin.

That name had nested somewhere behind his ribs since the night before. Now, it fluttered constantly. He had tried, truly, to move past it. To replace the absence with new laughter, new scents, new silences beside Taher. But the old wound wasn't healed – just bandaged.

He needed to confess.

Not to reclaim anything. Not to rewind time.

Just to finally let it out. For Jobin to know that Gokul had loved him. Deeply. Silently. Foolishly. Fully.

A gentle nudge from Lakshmiamma brought him back.

"Gokule?"

"Hm?"

“More chicken?” she asked, already reaching toward the bowl.

He blinked. “No, Ammamma. I’m full.”

She gave him a look – the kind that knew when someone wasn’t being fully honest – but nodded and leaned back.

After washing his hands and drying them on the old blue towel, Gokul stepped into the hallway. The scent of turmeric and coconut oil still clung to his fingers. He picked up his phone from the windowsill and typed quickly, before he changed his mind:

"Can we meet at the old pond? Now?”

Outside, the birds were loud with noon heat. Somewhere in the background, the news anchor's voice was still rising from the TV, but Gokul had already stepped out – toward the pond, toward Taher, and maybe... toward a bit of peace.

***

The breeze by the pond was gentler today. The kind that rustled leaves without urgency. Gokul walked slowly, taking his time with each step. His chappals scuffed the dry earth, and the sunlight flitted between the trees like shy glances.

There–he saw him.

Taher was already sitting on their usual rock, his feet barely touching the water. He looked... softer than usual.

His shoulders slouched slightly, a strand of hair curling against his forehead. He was being himself—truly himself—in a way he rarely let the world see. Just a bit more effeminate, a bit more real. Gokul noticed. He always did.

"You okay?" Gokul asked, gently, easing down next to him.

Taher nodded, but with a tired smile. "The festival took a toll, da. So much noise, so many people. I think I need one whole day just to sleep."

Gokul chuckled under his breath, but his voice was a little slower, more deliberate. "I called you because… I'm going back to Kochi. Just for a day or two."

Taher turned his face slowly, a flicker of worry brushing across his eyes. "Oh?"

"I need to meet Jobin. For real. I need to tell him what I feel—what I felt. Not to win him back… I know that's not happening. But I want him to know. To really know."

Taher was quiet. He shifted, his shoulder brushing gently against Gokul's. He didn't respond immediately. He just looked ahead—at the light skipping across the pond surface like ripples of an old memory.

Then he let out a slow, deep breath. "You should go. You'll feel lighter, Gokul. You need that."

Gokul looked at him, a silent thanks in his eyes.

Then—Taher leaned in and wrapped his arms around him. No words. No hesitations. Just a warm, firm embrace.

Gokul let himself melt into it—leaning against Taher's chest, his forehead resting against the familiar curve of his collarbone. That same scent again—like guava dried in the sun, soft and tangy and home. Gokul closed his eyes for a second longer than usual. He didn't know he needed this hug… until it happened.

After what felt like a small eternity, Taher gently pulled away. But his hand lingered on Gokul's shoulder for just a beat more.

"When you're back," Taher said, "I've got something for you."

Gokul's lips curled into a curious smile. "A surprise?"

Taher nodded, looking almost mischievous, almost shy. "I finished the drawing book. The one with my designs. All of them. I want you to be the first to see."

Gokul's eyes lit up. "Are you serious? I've been dying to see it!"

Taher smiled—a full, open, effeminate smile that softened his entire face. The kind he usually tucked away when others were around. But with Gokul, it stayed.

"Come back soon, okay?"

"I will," Gokul said.

And for that brief moment, under the shade of the Gulmohar treee by the pond, everything between them felt still, unspoken, and yet—so understood.

Chapter 11: Back to Where It Broke

The room was quiet except for the whir of the ceiling fan and the distant call of a koel. Gokul sat on the edge of his bed, staring at his phone. His fingers hovered for a moment before opening the chat again.

There it was.

Jobin: *"Yes daaa, when are you coming?"*

Simple. Casual. As if nothing had passed between them. As if they were still in the same school corridor, stealing time between bells.

Gokul typed back,

"By noon. Just for a day."

He placed the phone face-down on the bed, exhaled slowly, and pulled his small sling bag closer. His fingers carefully slipped in the new drawing book–the one he bought from the village. On the first page, two faceless boys sitting by a pond, feet dangling into the water.

He slid in his earphones, his power bank, a handkerchief that still smelled faintly of pond water and talcum. He stood up to zip the bag–when the door creaked open.

"Take this, monu."

Laksmiamma walked in, holding a bottle of jeera water and a small packets of *chakka uperi* and banana chips, warm and neatly folded.

Gokul smiled faintly. "Ammamma, I'm okay. It's just one day."

She placed it on the bed anyway, ignoring him, her saree pleats rustling softly. "One day also you'll need something to eat. Street food is full of oil. You'll get sick. Eat this once you reach."

He paused for a second, touched. "Thanks, ammamma."

She looked at him, that gaze only grandmothers have–where love is buried in fussing. "What's this sudden project, da? Why so Important?"

He hesitated for a breath. "Yeah... It's for a school project I left pending. Thought I'll just finish it and come back. I'll be back before night."

She didn't entirely believe him, but she didn't push. She walked over and touched his forehead gently. "Be careful. Don't skip meals. And wear your mask if there's dust."

Gokul leaned in and planted a kiss on her cheek, soft and smelled of coconut oil. She smiled and kissed him back on his forehead, as if sealing something unspoken.

Outside, Aravind Achachan was sitting in the easy chair, half-reading the newspaper, half-watching the road. His eyes lifted the moment he saw Gokul with the bag.

"Hmm... Going?"

"Just one day, achacha."

Achachan nodded, but his face had that slight heaviness he never tried to hide.

"I'll be back before sunset," Gokul reassured, and bent down to hug him. Achachan's arms didn't move at first—but then he gave in and held him close, warm and awkward.

Gokul pulled back and grinned. "Keep the best ripe mangoes ready when I'm back."

Achachan chuckled, "Then you better come back soon. Otherwise I'll eat them all."

Gokul laughed, slipped into his sandals, and stepped outside. The sky was clear, too clear. He paused at the gate and inhaled—one long breath. The kind you take when you don't know how the day will unfold.

He pulled out his phone again and typed a quick message to Taher.

"I've started."

And then he walked. Down the familiar lane, past the tamarind tree, beyond the cracked wall where moss always grew—towards something that had already begun shifting inside him.

***

The train rumbled on, the rhythm of the wheels oddly calming. Gokul sat by the window, elbow propped up, chin resting on his palm. The landscape blurred—little green patches, distant buildings, sleepy towns passing by in lazy sequence. His fingers nervously tapped on the edge of the window. He had read the same message on his phone at least three times—Jobin's "Yes daa, when are you coming?" But no new reply after he said he'd reach by noon.

The train curved slightly. A breeze drifted in.

And just like that, he was back there.

The corridor was half-shadowed, hot from the afternoon sun. Gokul sat on the window ledge with Vimal and Subin, textbooks open across their laps. The exam bell was a little while away, and the corridor buzzed with tension, last-minute questions, and quiet murmurs of forgotten facts.

"Da, photosynthesis equation?" Subin asked.

"C6H12O6 something something... carbon dioxide and water in, glucose and oxygen out," Gokul mumbled.

He wasn't really paying attention.

His eyes drifted—past the other groups, past the dusty green walls—to the spot near the water cooler, where Jobin stood. Laughing, animated, flipping through a notebook with a new circle of friends. There was a girl who always wore thick eyeliner. Jobin looked comfortable. Like he belonged there now.

Gokul looked down at his own notes, then back up again. A soft ache settled in his chest.

Last year around this time, he and Jobin would've been heads-down, locked into their last-minute revision. Sharing pens. Sharing answers. Whispering guesses of what'd come. Gokul used to pick only the important questions—because Jobin hated reading too much—and they would quiz each other while walking from class to the hall.

He remembered lending Jobin his scale once during a physics exam. And how Jobin would always forget his calculator. Gokul carried a spare, just for him.

He remembered Jobin leaning close, muttering, "Da, you think gravitation will come? I didn't study that chapter."

And Gokul replying, "It always does. I told you yesterday also."

They had been a team.

And now... he was just someone watching from the sidelines.

The corridor around him started to blur, a sting slowly crawling up behind his eyes.

"Da Goku, bell will ring soon, come on," Vimal nudged him.

Gokul blinked. The present came rushing back like water from a broken pipe.

***

The train gave a sudden jolt. A sharp whistle. And then slowed.

Gokul sat upright. The station signs read **Ernakulam Junction.**

Kochi.

He grabbed his bag, stepped down, and onto the platform. The familiar smell of fried snacks and train oil filled the air. He looked around–just the usual crowd. Nothing extraordinary.

He checked his phone.

Still no new message.

He called. The phone rang twice.

"Hello?"

It was Jobin's voice. Crisp. The same.

"Hey... I just reached," Gokul said, trying to sound light.

"Ah, okay. Where are you now?"

"Platform 4. I thought I'll just go straight to the café."

There was a pause. Then, "Cool. See you there."

The line cut. No added "drive safe" or "glad you came." Just clean, flat acceptance.

Gokul stared at the phone screen for a second before pocketing it. He stepped out into the sun, flagged an auto.

"To Kadavanthra Junction.

The auto driver nodded and started the engine.

As the auto curved past the dusty roads of Kochi, Gokul gripped his sketchbook tight inside his bag. His drawing of two faceless boys suddenly felt like a mirror.

Gokul thought of that old café–the one with wooden benches, and puffs that were always a little too oily. But it was their place.

Where ideas were born. Where laughter came easy. Where things were still simple.

He didn't know what this meeting would bring. He wasn't expecting apologies. Or miracles.

But maybe, just maybe, he could walk away this time knowing he said what he needed to.

And that was enough.

Chapter 12: The Little Secret

The café hadn't changed. Same grey walls, same glass jars filled with stale pastries by the counter. Gokul reached first. He slid into the corner seat—their seat—and texted:

"I'm here."

A reply came in almost instantly.

"Just around the corner daa."

He smiled faintly. Gokul placed the order before Jobin arrived—two egg puffs and two fresh limes. Just like old times. Just like back when their laughter filled this space.

The waiter brought the plates as Jobin walked in.

Gokul stood up. He almost couldn't believe the figure that entered. Jobin looked... older, sharper. The once curly locks were trimmed down to a short, crisp cut. His jawline had toughened. His body filled his t-shirt like it was part of him.

But the smile—that old, half-smile—was still the same.

They hugged. It was warm, tight, familiar in scent. Jobin still smelled like afternoons after school: sweat, faint cologne, and the sun. But something was off. This time, the embrace felt like borrowed nostalgia. Too measured. Too brief.

They sat.

"How are things?" Jobin asked casually.

Gokul nodded. "Good. I'm on a break. Staying at ammamma's place... in the village."

Jobin looked around the café. "Same place, huh. Been a while."

Gokul gestured at the plate. "Eat your puff before it gets cold."

Jobin smirked, waved it off. "Can't, da. Diet. Trying to stay shredded these days. Gym every morning."

Gokul didn't respond. He smiled politely, but something inside him folded. The puff sat there uneaten. The air around them slowly thickened with unsaid things.

Gokul looked down into his bag. His sketchbook was half out, the edges frayed. He peeked at it, the page where two faceless boys sat by the pond. He shut it quickly. That wasn't the moment.

"I'm going to ask you directly," he said.

Jobin blinked. "Okay..."

"Why did you just... stop being my friend?"

There was no anger in his voice. Just a quiet ache, like an old wound surfacing in sunlight.

"There was a time," Gokul continued, "when even the smallest thing–you'd come running to tell me. And suddenly, I became someone you walked past in corridors."

Jobin sighed. "Da, you're overthinking it. You know how it is. New groups, different vibes... But we're still the same, no?"

"No," Gokul said softly. "We're not. You stopped showing up. You stopped looking at me."

There was silence. Jobin looked around, uncomfortable.

Gokul took a sip of his fresh lime. His hands were shaking. But his voice stayed steady.

"There's something you should know," he said, looking at Jobin. "I know it won't change anything, but I need to say it."

Jobin's gaze held his for the first time that afternoon.

"I loved you," Gokul said.

The words didn't echo. They just hung there between them, like mist.

"I'm gay," he continued, "and I loved you more than a friend. I don't expect anything from you. I just wanted you to know."

Jobin shifted in his seat. His face didn't change much. Maybe just his eyes.

"You know I'm straight, right?" he said after a pause.

"I know," Gokul replied. "I never wanted anything else. I just... missed my friend."

Jobin looked away. Maybe embarrassed. Maybe confused.

"I wanted your presence. That was enough," Gokul said, standing up. "But it's okay. You can keep that too."

He smiled faintly, adjusted his sling bag.

"All the best, da. For everything."

Jobin gave a smirk. That same smirk. Like he didn't know what else to do with his face. "You too, da," he said quietly.

Gokul walked out.

He didn't cry. He didn't even feel like it. He just got into the nearest auto, gave the station name, and leaned back.

The auto weaved through the busy streets of Kochi. Posters, honks, sun glare through dusty windshields. It felt distant.

At the station, he caught the next train heading back. He didn't care about timing or seats. He stood by the door as the train rushed through fields, brick factories, and green blurs of home.

The wind hit his face. Gokul pulled out his sketchbook again.

The drawing.

Two boys. Sitting by a pond.

He looked at them again.

It wasn't him and Jobin.

It was him and Taher.

It always had been.

The more he stared at the faceless boys in the sketch, the clearer the faces became. Not Jobin's sharp jawline or his expensive cologne. But Taher's—his soft eyes, the gentleness stitched into every move, the way his hair curled slightly when wet, the way he adjusted his mundu around Gokul's waist with quiet care, the way he grinned, crooked and bashful, when embarrassed. The way he always, always made space for Gokul. In conversation. In silence. In memory.

It was the cycle rides, Gokul on the front rail, wind in his hair, and Taher behind, firm and steady. That unmistakable scent—sun-dried guava and something faintly floral—wrapped around him like a spell. The scent that clung to Gokul's shirt long after the ride was over, long after the laughter faded into the hum of the village.

It was the festival night, both in mundus, hands brushing, hearts thumping quietly under the stars. Taher, anxious in the crowd, leaning into Gokul's embrace, letting his breath steady against Gokul's neck. That moment—where his body loosened, trusting, warm—etched into Gokul's skin like sunlight.

It was the mangoes by the stream, the hidden smiles, the playful splashes in the water, the way Taher called him *da* like it meant more than just familiarity—like it meant belonging. Like it meant love.

Taher never had to say it. It was in his touch. In the way he waited. In the way he listened, really listened. In the tear he shed when Gokul gifted him the sketchbook. In the softness of his laugh when Gokul stole a bite of his uzhunnu vada. In the way he said, "You don't know what gems are already in front of you."

And now Gokul knew.

Jobin had been a longing. A wound that festered in silence.

But Taher?

Taher was healing.

Taher was home.

Gokul looked at the fields racing past. His fingers grazed the edges of the drawing book.

His heart was still thudding.

He whispered to himself, barely audible over the wind–

"It was always you, Taher."

And the wind carried it forward, ahead of the train, as if taking it to where it needed to go first.

Home.

To him.

Chapter 13:
The Scent in the Wind

The auto rattled through the winding roads of Palakkad, the late evening sun stretching long shadows across the path. Gokul clutched his sling bag tightly, heart racing. His eyes scanned the familiar trees, the crooked milestones, the turn near Balan chettan's tea stall. Almost home. Almost there.

He didn't wait for the auto to stop completely before jumping out. The metal gates creaked open as he pushed them in haste. The warm smell of rice water and curry leaves still lingered in the air—his home still smelled like love.

And there she was.

Laxmiamma stood on the edge of the veranda, one hand resting on the wooden pillar, eyes waiting. But something in her face had changed. There was no smile. No teasing "Mone, where's my mango?" like she usually would say.

"Ammamme..." Gokul's voice broke the stillness. "Where's Achachan?"

Laxmiamma took a deep breath. Her lips trembled.

"He's... at Taher's house."

Gokul stopped. His breath caught.

"What? Why?" He stepped closer. "What happened?"

Laxmiamma looked at him, her eyes glassy, swollen. "Taher is no more, Gokule."

The words fell like a slab of stone across his chest.

He blinked.

"What?" His voice cracked.

"Taher passed away... today afternoon. He was taken to the medical college in the morning. He had a tumour. In his colon. It was undiagnosed. It spread... It got worse. They couldn't..."

"No." Gokul stepped back.

His bag slid off his shoulder, hitting the tiled floor with a thud.

"No... No, no, no. What are you saying?"

Tears streamed down his face before he realised it. He pressed his hands to his ears, as if trying to shut out the words.

"No, Ammamma... this can't... he was just—he was just texting me yesterday! He was fine. We were talking. We were..."

He dropped to the floor, sitting on the cool cement, his body shaking.

The scent.

That warm sun-dried guava scent—he could still smell it in his shirt. He could still feel Taher's arms around him, the lingering press of their last hug. The sketchbook. The promise.

"When you're back, I've got a surprise for you."

He sobbed now, like a child—raw, broken.

"I didn't know... I didn't know he was unwell... why didn't he tell me?"

Laxmiamma walked slowly over to him, lowered herself beside him, pulled him into her arms.

"They didn't tell anyone. His parents and him took it lightly. But they didn't know how bad it was."

Gokul cried harder, chest aching, breath shattered. The floodgates of every moment they had shared opened wide.

The cycle rides.

The stream.

The mundu he helped him tie.

The pond.

The festival night, standing hand in hand.

His softness. His strength.

His eyes.

His scent.

And now... just silence.

Laxmiamma gently rocked him.

"Cry, mone. It's okay. Let it out."

Gokul shook in her arms.

"I never told him. I never told him what he meant to me. I was going to. I had decided. I was going to tell him everything..."

Laxmiamma wiped his cheeks with the edge of her sari.

"He knew, Gokul. Sometimes you don't need words. Some people just... know."

He leaned into her, breaking all over again.

Outside, the sun was bleeding into dusk. A faint breeze passed through the trees, bringing with it the scent of mango blossoms, wet earth... and something sweet.

Gokul closed his eyes.

He could almost smell him.

Almost feel him.

But now, he was just a memory. A scent in the wind.

And Gokul—wasn't ready to let go.

***

The sky had turned a dull ochre when Gokul reached Taher's home. The sun, low and red, painted everything in sorrowed light.

There was a muffled silence all around, broken only by the soft sounds of sobbing inside the house. Taher's mother sat on the floor near the entrance, clutching a towel, her eyes red and hollow. His younger sister rested her head on their mother's lap, crying without a sound, as if her grief had sunk too deep to make noise. A few women from the neighbourhood sat around them reciting gentle verses from the Qur'an, whispering prayers into the air, their voices like soft winds through mourning leaves.

Gokul stood at the threshold for a moment, frozen. Then, as if something snapped, he entered slowly.

Taher's father was at the far end of the room, pacing. A man trying hard not to break. His back was straight, arms crossed, jaw clenched—but his eyes betrayed him. They were bloodshot, wet, and tired of pretending. He nodded once when he saw Gokul, but said nothing.

And then, in the centre of the room, wrapped in a clean white kaffan, lay Taher.

Gokul moved forward, legs trembling, and knelt down beside him. His fingers shook as he touched the fabric over Taher's cheeks, and then slowly, he peeled it back–just for a second.

Cold.

His skin, once so warm and soft with laughter, now lay still. Eyes closed, lips gently parted as if mid-thought, mid-smile, mid-life.

Gokul broke.

He leaned in, placed his forehead against Taher's, and wept. Not loud, not wailing. Just tears, rushing, falling, crashing like waves that had held too long.

"I'm here," he whispered. "I came back... I kept my promise."

It was time.

The men from the mosque arrived to prepare the body for Janazah. The ritual bath–Ghusl–had already been done by close male relatives and neighbours. Taher had been shrouded properly, his face shown one last time for those who loved him. Now, the body was to be taken to the mosque.

Gokul stood among the men, his sleeves rolled up. No one stopped him.

He helped lift the body, feeling the real weight now—not just of Taher, but of absence, of all that could never be said. The cotton shroud pressed against his shoulder as they carried him down the narrow street, toward the mosque lit with a soft golden glow.

Taher's father walked beside them in silence.

At the mosque, they laid the janazah on the floor facing the qibla. The congregation lined up—shoulder to shoulder—and offered the Janazah prayer. It was short, solemn, and final. A prayer for mercy, for forgiveness, for peace in the next world.

Gokul whispered his own prayer quietly, eyes closed.

When the prayer ended, they lifted the body again—this time, toward the cemetery.

The final walk.

The grave had been dug in the traditional manner, deep and facing Mecca. As the white shroud was lowered gently into the earth, Gokul stood back, his fists clenched.

Two men stepped in and tilted Taher gently onto his right side, facing the qibla. They placed a few clumps of moist sand beneath his head. Another man began pouring soil into the grave, whispering "Bismillah wa ala millati Rasulillah"—in the name of God and in the faith of the Messenger of God.

Gokul watched, still. Unmoving.

The grave filled slowly. With every handful of earth, the world felt emptier.

When it was done, someone placed a simple wooden marker at the head. The name hadn't been carved yet. It was too soon.

Gokul stepped forward one last time. The scent of guava in the sun was no longer there. But the memory was. And in that moment, he whispered the only words he could muster.

"I'll love you... always."

And he stood there until the light dimmed into night.

Chapter 14: The Silence that Followed

The sky was muted, the kind of grey that lingered without promise. The village air carried a silence too heavy for birdsong. Gokul lay quietly on his mother's lap, his head turned toward the open window. Latha slowly combed her fingers through his hair, the way she used to when he was sick as a child. Only now, it was a different kind of ache—this one didn't have a name, nor a medicine.

She didn't say much. Just hummed an old song under her breath, broken at places by her own emotion. He could feel her breath catch each time he shifted and she realised her son had grown so much, yet still looked for her lap when life got too hard.

From the courtyard, his father's voice called gently. "Gokul... come with me."

Gokul stood slowly. Latha gave his hand a soft squeeze before he stepped out.

They walked under the old mango tree—its leaves rustled like old relatives murmuring. Aravind achachan's chair creaked in the distance, where he sat quietly.

His father, Suresh, stood beside him, looking at the low-hanging mangoes above. "They've ripen early this year," he said, breaking the silence.

Gokul didn't respond. He just looked up and watched the light dancing through the gaps in the branches.

Suresh exhaled. "When I was in college," he began, "I had a friend named Rakesh. Crazy fellow. We did everything together. Slept in the same room, skipped classes, failed a few subjects too." A soft laugh, with the heaviness of memory. "He was the kind of friend who didn't need words to know what I was thinking."

Gokul turned slightly.

"One night," Suresh continued, "he went out to get food. A bike accident. That's it. Gone." His voice cracked. "Just like that."

A pause. Then he looked at Gokul.

"I couldn't believe it. Spent the rest of the semester with long hair, a full beard... didn't touch a trimmer. Ma thought I'd lost it." He smiled faintly. "Maybe I had."

He placed a hand gently on Gokul's shoulder.

"Losing people... it breaks something in you. But that's life. No notice. No warnings. We never know who's going to stay, who's going to leave."

He turned and looked at his own father, Aravind Achachan, now sitting still on the veranda, gazing toward them. His newspaper lay forgotten in his lap.

"And yet," Suresh said, voice soft, "somehow, we learn to carry them... not with tears, but with the love they left behind."

Gokul's eyes stung. He wanted to scream. To say it loud—that Taher wasn't just a friend. That he was more. So much more. That Taher's laughter, his scent, the warmth of his hands—none of it was ordinary.

But he couldn't say it.

His throat tightened, the words suffocated.

Instead, he just moved forward and fell into his father's arms.

Suresh held him tightly. No questions. No pressure.

Just an embrace. A father's embrace.

And there, under the mango tree, where the sun pierced through green, Gokul cried—not loudly, not messily. Just tears, tracing down his cheeks like quiet acknowledgements of a love that never got to become.

And he let himself be held.

Because sometimes, that's all grief asks for.

***

The sky was a quiet shade of grey when Gokul began packing. His bag was already zipped, but it still felt incomplete—like something was missing.

He hugged Laxmiamma first. She held him for a long time, her hands rubbing his back gently, as though memorising the shape of her grandson once more. "No worries, you'll be okay." she whispered.

Aravind Achachan walked over and gave him a tight embrace. Stronger than usual. Then, with trembling lips, he placed a kiss on Gokul's forehead. That was new.

Gokul didn't speak much. Just nodded and smiled a tired smile. He picked up his bag, slung it across his shoulder, and looked at his father.

"Achan... can I go see Taher's house once... before we leave?"

Suresh paused, then gave a gentle nod. "Go, mone. Take your time."

Gokul walked quickly through the narrow winding paths, past the rubber trees and jackfruit stands. Everything felt still. Too still. The house, Taher's house, his cycle leaning aginst the wall ownerless, like it always had—but it felt different now. Hollow.

The front door was ajar. Inside, silence.

Taher's mother was lying sideways on the cot in the hall, eyes open, tears long dried on her cheeks. She looked at Gokul and offered a tired smile. "Come in, mone."

He sat near her. She reached for his hand.

"His father... he's not home," she said, her voice barely a whisper. "He can't sit in this house anymore... says it suffocates him."

She looked away and wiped her eyes. "It's our fault, Gokul. We thought it was just his diet. Or gas. We didn't think to go to the city hospital. We delayed. We..." her voice cracked.

Gokul didn't know what to say. He just held her hand tighter. That was all he could do.

From the kitchen, Taher's sister was quietly preparing lunch. The smell of onions frying, mixed with something tangy—maybe tamarind—lingered in the air. Familiar, warm, and unbearably heartbreaking.

Gokul stood up and asked softly, "Can I... go to his room?"

She nodded. "Of course. You know the way."

He walked down the narrow corridor. The room was dimly lit, a faint stream of sunlight seeping through the curtain. The bed was made, but slightly creased. The air still carried *him*—the soft scent of sun-dried guava, but faint now. Distant.

Gokul sat down on the edge of the bed. The mattress sank beneath him, and he felt the ghost of Taher beside him. He turned slowly, reached for the cupboard, and opened it.

There, neatly folded, was one of Taher's shirts.

Gokul took it into his hands and brought it close to his face.

That scent again.

He closed his eyes and let himself cry, softly, like a child who'd dropped something too precious to fix. He buried his face into the fabric, wishing he could fold into time and press himself against Taher once more.

Then, out of the corner of his eye, he saw it.

The sketchbook.

The surprise Taher never got to show him.

He opened the first page.

A dress. Then another. Then sarees, then kurtas, fusion wear, and gowns that looked like they belonged in Milan or Paris. Each sketch more confident than the last—notes scribbled in the corners, thread suggestions, accessory pairings.

Taher was going to be a name.

And then, the final page.

Gokul froze.

There he was.

Gokul, standing tall in a regal wedding suit. Navy blue, his favourite. Gold embroidery lined the sleeves and collar. A matching stole across the shoulder. His hair was styled, and his eyes were sparkling. The caption under the page read in delicate cursive:

"For him, always."

Gokul's hands trembled. The tears came again, heavier this time. He turned away from the page, holding the book to his chest.

He wanted to scream. To call Taher back just once. Just to say thank you. Just to say I love you too.

He didn't need a reply.

But now he knew.

Taher had loved him. Not just in quiet gestures, not just in scents and sketches and tea stalls. But with all of him.

It was real. It was theirs. And now, it would live only in Gokul.

The forbidden love. The beautiful, soft love.

And he held it, like one holds fire—burning, precious, and gone.

Gokul gently closed the sketchbook, brushing his fingers once across the cover like it was skin. He looked around Taher's room one last time, drinking in every little corner – the crooked stack of books, the half-used bottle of coconut oil, the fan that hummed on low. Then, with steady hands, he slipped the sketchbook into his sling bag.

He was taking it with him.

The memory of Taher. The dream Taher once held. The love stitched between each page.

***

By the time they reached the car, the sun had begun to dip. Orange and pink spilled across the sky. His mother sat in the back seat beside him, her hands softly resting on his thigh. His father drove in silence, eyes fixed on the road ahead but heart still somewhere in the village.

No one spoke much.

Even the wind outside the car window seemed to move slower now, like it knew what they carried with them.

Gokul leaned his head against the windowpane, his breath leaving little clouds. Then slowly, he opened his own sketchbook, the one he had packed before leaving the village – the one with faceless boys by a pond.

Only now, they weren't faceless anymore.

The lines were clearer. One boy had hair pulled back messily and a tilt to his posture – soft, like sunlight through trees. The other sat closer, sketchbook resting on his knees, a shy half-smile caught between admiration and wonder.

Taher and Gokul. By the pond. Under the gulmohar tree. Forever.

Gokul smiled faintly, tracing the outline of Taher's eyes with the tip of his pencil.

He didn't need to say anything. The silence between the pages was loud enough.

And just like that, with a sketchbook on his lap and a heart heavy but full, Gokul carried Taher home – not just in a bag, but in him.

Always.